PEG WOFFINGTON.

A NOVEL.

BY CHARLES READE,

AUTHOR OF "CHRISTIE JOHNSTONE."

BOSTON:

TICKNOR AND FIELDS.

M DCCC LV.

TO

T. TAYLOR, ESQ.,

MY FRIEND, AND COADJUTOR IN THE COMEDY

OF

"MASKS AND FACES,"

TO WHOM THE READER OWES MUCH OF THE BEST MATTER IN THIS TALE:

AND TO THE MEMORY OF MARGARET WOFFINGTON,

FALSELY *summed up* UNTIL TO-DAY,

THIS

Dramatic Story"

IS INSCRIBED BY

CHARLES READE.

LONDON,
DECEMBER 15, 1852.

PEG WOFFINGTON.

CHAPTER I.

About the middle of the last century, at eight o'clock in the evening, in a large but poor apartment, a man was slumbering on a rough couch. His rusty and worn suit of black was of a piece with his uncarpeted room, the deal table of home manufacture, and its slim, unsnuffed candle.

The man was Triplet, scene painter, actor, and writer of sanguinary plays, in which what ought to be, viz., truth, plot, situation, and dialogue, were not; and what ought not to be, were: *scilicet,* small talk, big talk, fops, ruffians, and ghosts.

His three mediocrities fell so short of one talent, that he was sometimes *impransus.*

He slumbered, but uneasily. The dramatic

author was uppermost, and his "Demon of the Hayloft" hung upon the thread of popular favor.

On his uneasy slumber entered from the theatre Mrs. Triplet.

She was a lady who in one respect fell behind her husband. She lacked his variety in ill-doing, but she recovered herself by doing her one thing a shade worse than he did any of his three. She was what is called, in grim sport, an actress; she had just cast her mite of discredit on royalty by playing the Queen, and had trundled home the moment the breath was out of her royal body. She came in rotatory with fatigue, and fell, gristle, into a chair; she wrenched from her brow a diadem, and eyed it with contempt; took from her pocket a sausage, and contemplated it with respect and affection, placed it in a frying pan on the fire, and entered her bed room, meaning to don a loose wrapper, and dethrone herself into comfort.

But the poor woman was shot walking by Morpheus, and subsided altogether; for dramatic performances, amusing and exciting to youth seated in the pit, convey a certain weariness to those bright beings who sparkle on the stage for bread and cheese.

Royalty disposed of still left its trail of events. The sausage began to "spit." The sound was hardly out of its body when poor Triplet writhed like a worm on a hook. "Spitter, spittest," went the sausage. Triplet groaned, and at last his inarticulate murmurs became words: "That's right, pit; now, that is so reasonable to condemn a poor fellow's play before you have heard it out." Then, with a change of tone, "Tom," muttered he, "they are losing their respect for spectres; if they do, hunger will make a ghost of me." Next he fancied the clown, or somebody, had got into his ghost's costume.

"Dear," said the poor dreamer, "the clown makes a very pretty spectre, with his ghastly white face, and his blood-boltered cheeks and nose. I never saw the fun of a clown before. No, no, no! it is not the clown; it is worse, much worse! O dear! ugh!" and Triplet rolled off the couch like Richard the Third. He sat a moment on the floor with a finger in each eye; and then, finding he was neither daubing, ranting, nor deluging earth with "acts," he accused himself of indolence, and sat down to write a small tale of blood and bombast; he took his seat at the deal table with some alacrity, for he had recently made a discovery.

How to write well, *rien que cela.*

"First, think in as homely a way as you can; next, shove your pen under the thought, and lift it by polysyllables to the true level of fiction;" (when done, find a publisher, if you can.) "This," said Triplet, "insures common sense to your ideas, which does pretty well for a basis," said Triplet, apologetically, "and elegance to the dress they wear." Triplet then, casting his eyes round in search of such actual circumstances as could be incorporated on this plan with fiction, began to work thus: —

TRIPLET'S FACTS.	TRIPLET'S FICTION.
A farthing dip is on the table.	A solitary candle cast its pale gleams around.
It wants snuffing.	Its elongated wick betrayed an owner steeped in oblivion.
He jumped up, and snuffed it with his fingers; burned his fingers, and swore a little.	He rose languidly, and trimmed it with an instrument that he had by his side for that purpose, and muttered a silent ejaculation.

Before, however, the mole Triplet could undermine literature and level it with the dust, various interruptions and divisions broke in upon his design, and *sic nos servavit* Apollo. As he wrote the last sentence a loud rap came to his door. A servant in livery brought him a note from Mr. Vane, dated Covent Garden. Triplet's eyes sparkled; he bustled, wormed himself into a less rusty coat, and started off to the Theatre Royal, Covent Garden.

In those days the artists of the pen and the brush ferreted patrons, instead of aiming to be indispensable to the public, the only patron worth a single gesture of the quill.

Mr. Vane had conversed with Triplet, that is, let Triplet talk to him in a coffee house; and Triplet, the most sanguine of unfortunate men, had already built a series of expectations upon that interview, when this note arrived. Leaving him on his road from Lambeth to Covent Garden, we must introduce more important personages.

Mr. Vane was a wealthy gentleman from Shropshire, whom business had called to London four months ago, and now pleasure detained. Business still occupied the letters he sent now and then to his native county ; but it had ceased to occupy the writer. He was a man of learning and taste, as times went ; and his love of the arts had taken him some time before our tale to the theatres, then the resort of all who pretended to taste ; and it was thus he had become fascinated by Mrs. Woffington, a lady of great beauty, and a comedian high in favor with the town.

The first night he saw her was an epoch in the history of this gentleman's mind. He had learning and refinement, and he had not great practical experience ; and such men are most open to impression from the stage. He saw a being, all grace and bright nature, move like a goddess among the stiff puppets of the scene ; her glee and her pathos were equally catching ; she held a golden key at which all the doors of the heart flew open. Her face, too, was as full of goodness as intelligence ; it was like no other face. The heart bounded to meet it.

He rented a box at her theatre. He was there every night before the curtain drew up ; and, I am sorry to say, he at last took half a dislike to Sunday — Sunday, " which knits up the ravelled slave of care" Sunday, "tired Nature's sweet restorer," because on Sunday there was no Peg Woffington. At first he regarded her as a being of another sphere, an incarnation of poetry and art; but by degrees his secret aspirations became bolder. She was a woman; there were men who knew her; some of them inferior to him in position, and, he flattered himself, in mind. He had even heard a tale against her character. To him her face was its confutation, and he knew how loose-tongued is calumny; but still —!

At last, one day, he sent her a letter, unsigned. This letter expressed his admiration of her talent in warm but respectful terms. The writer told her it had become necessary to his heart to return her in some way his thanks for the land of enchantment to which she had introduced him. Soon after this choice flowers found their way to her dressing room every night, and now and then verses and precious stones mingled with her roses and eglantine. And O, how he watched the great actress's eye all the night! how he tried to discover whether she looked oftener towards his box than the corresponding box on the other side of the house!

Did she notice him, or did she not? What a point gained if she was conscious of his nightly attendance! She would feel he was a friend, not a mere auditor. He was jealous of the pit, on whom Mrs. Woffington lavished her smiles without measure.

At last, one day he sent her a wreath of flowers, and implored her, if any word he had said to her had pleased or interested her, to wear this wreath that night. After he had done this he trembled; he had courted a decision, when, perhaps, his safety lay in patience and time. She made her *entrée*; he turned cold as she glided into sight from the prompter's side; he raised his eyes slowly and fearfully from her feet to her head; her head was bare, wreathed only by its own rich, glossy honors. "Fool," thought he, "to think she would hang frivolities upon that glorious head for me." Yet his disappointment told him he had really hoped it. He would not have sat out the play but for a leaden incapacity of motion that seized him.

The curtain drew up for the fifth act, and — could he believe his eyes? — Mrs. Woffington stood upon the stage with his wreath upon her graceful head. She took away his breath. She spoke the epilogue, and as the curtain fell, she lifted her eyes, he thought, to his box, and made him a distinct, queen-like courtesy. His heart fluttered to his mouth, and he walked home on wings and tiptoe. In short—

Mrs. Woffington, as an actress, justified a portion of this enthusiasm. She was one of the truest artists of her day; a fine lady in her hands was a lady, with the genteel affectation of a gentlewoman, not a harlot's affectation, which is simply and without exaggeration what the stage commonly gives us for a fine lady; an old woman in her hands was a thorough woman, thoroughly old, not a cackling young person of epicene gender. She played Sir Harry Wildair like a man, which is how he ought to be played, (or, which is better still, not at all,) so that Garrick acknowledged her as a male rival, and abandoned the part he no longer monopolized.

Now, it very, very rarely happens that a woman of her age is high enough in art and knowledge to do these things. In players, vanity cripples art at every step. The young actress who is not a Woffington aims to display herself by means of her part, which is vanity; not to raise her part by sinking herself in it, which is art. It has been my misfortune to see ——, and ——, and ——, and ——, et ceteras, play the man; nature, forgive them if you can, for art never will; they never reached any idea more manly than a steady resolve to exhibit the points of a woman with greater ferocity than they could in a gown. But consider, ladies, a man is not the meanest of the brute creation; so how can he be an unwomanly female. This sort of actress aims not to give her author's creation to the public, but to trot out the person instead of the creation, and show sots what a calf it has — and is.

Vanity, vanity! all is vanity! Mesdames les Charlatanes.

Margaret Woffington was of another mould. She played the ladies of high comedy with grace, distinction, and delicacy. But in Sir Harry Wildair she parted with a woman's mincing foot and tongue, and played the man in a style large, spirited, and *élancé*. As Mrs. Day, (committee,) she painted wrinkles on her lovely face so honestly, that she was taken for threescore; and she carried out the design with voice and person, and did a vulgar old woman to the life. She disfigured her own beauties to show the beauty of her art; in a word, she was an artist. It does not follow she was the greatest artist that ever breathed; far from it. Mr. Vane was carried to this notion by passion and ignorance.

On the evening of our tale he was at his post, patiently sitting out one of these sanguinary discourses our rude forefathers thought were tragic plays. *Sedet æternumque Sedebit Infelix Theseus,* because Mrs. Woffington is to speak the epilogue.

These epilogues were curiosities of the human mind; they whom, just to ourselves and *them,* we call our *forbears,* had an idea their blood and bombast were not ridiculous enough in themselves; so when the curtain had fallen on the *débris* of the *dramatis personæ,* and of common sense, they sent on an actress to turn all the sentiment so laboriously acquired into a jest.

To insist that nothing good or beautiful shall be carried safe from a play out into the street was the bigotry of English horse play. Was a Lucretia the heroine of the tragedy, she was careful in the epilogue to speak like Messalina. Did a king's mistress come to hunger and repentance, she disinfected all the *petites maîtresses* in the house of the moral, by assuring them that sin is a joke, repentance a greater, and that she individually was ready for either if they would but cry, laugh, and pay. Then the audience used to laugh; and if they did not, lo! the manager, actor, and author of heroic tragedy were exceeding sorrowful.

Whilst sitting attèndance on the epilogue, Mr. Vane had nothing to distract him from the congregation but a sanguinary sermon in five heads; so his eyes roved over the pews, and presently he became aware of a familiar face watching him closely. The gentleman to whom it belonged, finding himself recognized, left his seat, and a minute later Sir Charles Pomander entered Mr. Vane's box.

This Sir Charles Pomander was a gentleman of vice: pleasure he called it. Mr. Vane had made his acquaintance two years ago in Shropshire. Sir Charles, who husbanded every thing except his soul, had turned himself out to grass for a month. His object was, by roast mutton, bread, with some little flour in it, air, water, temperance, chastity, and peace, to be enabled to take a deeper plunge into impurities of food and morals.

A few nights ago, unseen by Mr. Vane, he had observed him in the theatre. An ordinary man would have gone at once and shaken hands with him; but this was not an ordinary man, this was a diplomatist. First of all, he said to himself, "What is this man doing here?" Then he soon discovered this man must be in love with some actress; then it became his business to know who she was; this, too, soon betrayed itself. Then it became more than ever Sir Charles's business to know whether Mrs. Woffington returned the sentiment — and here his penetration was at fault for the moment; he determined, however, to discover.

Mr. Vane then received his friend all unsuspicious how that friend had been skinning him with his eyes for some time past. After the usual compliments had passed between two gentlemen who had been hand and glove for a month, and forgotten each other's existence for two years, Sir Charles, still keeping in view his design, said, —

"Let us go upon the stage." The fourth act had just concluded.

"Go upon the stage!" said Mr. Vane. "What! where she — I mean among the actors?"

"Yes; come into the greenroom. There are one or two people of reputation there: I will introduce you to them if you please."

"Go upon the stage!" Why, if it had been proposed to him to go to heaven he would not have been more astonished. He was too astonished at first to realize the full beauty of the arrangement, by means of which he might be within a yard of Mrs. Woffington, might feel her dress rustle past him, might speak to her, might drink her voice fresh from her lips almost before it mingled with meaner air. Silence gives consent, and Mr. Vane, though he thought a great deal, said nothing; so Pomander rose, and they left the boxes together. He led the way to the stage door, which was opened obsequiously to him. They then passed through a dismal passage, and suddenly emerged upon that scene of enchantment, the *stage* — a dirty platform, encumbered on all sides with piles of scenery in flats. They threaded their way through rusty velvet actors and fustian carpenters, and entered the greenroom. At the door of this magic chamber Vane trembled, and half wished he could retire. They entered; his apprehension gave way to disappointment; she was not there. Collecting himself, he was presently introduced to a smart, janty, and, to do him justice, *distingué* old beau. This was Colley Cibber, Esq., poet laureate, and retired actor and dramatist — a gentleman who is entitled to a word or two.

This Cibber was the only actor since Shakspeare's time who had both acted and written well. Pope's personal resentment misleads the reader of English poetry as to Cibber's real place among the wits of the day.

The man's talent was dramatic, not didactic, or epic, or pastoral. Pope was not so deep in the drama as in other matters, and Cibber was one of its luminaries. He wrote some of the best comedies of his day. He also succeeded where Dryden, for lack of true dramatic taste, failed. He tampered successfully with Shak speare. Colley Cibber's version of "Richard the Third" is impudent, and slightly larcenic, but it is marvellously effective. It has stood a century, and probably will stand forever; and the most admired passages, in what literary humbugs, who pretend they know Shakspeare by the closet, not the stage, accept as Shakspeare's "Richard," are Cibber's.

Mr. Cibber was now in private life, a mild edition of his own Lord Foppington; he had none of the snob fop, as represented on our conventional stage; nobody ever had and lived. He was in tolerably good taste; but he went ever gold laced, highly powdered, scented, and diamonded, dispensing graceful bows, praises of whoever had the good luck to be dead, and satire of all who were here to enjoy it.

Mr. Vane, to whom the drama had now become the golden branch of letters, looked with some awe on this veteran, for he had seen many Woffingtons. He fell soon upon the subject nearest his heart. He asked Mr. Cibber what he thought of Mrs. Woffington. The old gentleman thought well of the young lady's talent, especially her comedy. "In tragedy," said he, "she imitates Mademoiselle Dumesnil, of the Théâtre Français, and confounds the stage rhetorician with the actress." The next question was not so fortunate. "Did you ever see so great and true an actress, upon the whole?"

Mr. Cibber opened his eyes, a slight flush came into his wash-leather face, and he replied, "I have not only seen many equal, many superior to her, but I have seen some half dozen who would have eaten her up and spit her out again, and not known they had done any thing out of the way."

Here Pomander soothed the veteran's dudgeon by explaining in dulcet tones that his friend was not long from Shropshire, and —. The critic interrupted him, and bade him not dilute the excuse.

Now, Mr. Vane had as much to say as either of them, but he had not the habit, which dramatic folks have, of carrying his whole bank in his cheek pocket; so they quenched him for two minutes. But lovers are not silenced; he soon returned to the attack. He dwelt on the grace, the ease, and freshness, the intelligence, the universal beauty of Mrs. Woffington. Pomander sneered, to draw him out. Cibber smiled with good natured superiority. This nettled the young gentleman; he fired up; his handsome countenance glowed; he turned Demosthenes for her he loved One advantage he had over both Cibber and Pomander — a fair stock of classical learning. On this he now drew.

"Other actors and actresses," said he, "are monotonous in voice, monotonous in action; but Mrs. Woffington's delivery has the compass and variety of nature, and her movements are free from the stale uniformity that distinguishes artifice from art. The others seem to me to have but two dreams of grace; a sort of crawling on stilts is their motion, and an angular stiffness their repose." He then cited the most famous statues of antiquity, and quoted situations in plays where, by her fine dramatic instinct, Mrs. Woffington, he said, threw her person into postures similar to these, and of equal beauty; not that she strikes attitudes like the rest, but she melts from one beautiful statue into another; and if sculptors could gather from her immortal graces, painters, too, might take from her face the beauties that belong of right to passion and thought, and orators might revive their withered art, and learn from those golden lips the music of old Athens, that quelled tempestuous mobs, and princes drunk with victory.

Much as this was, he was going to say more, ever so much more; but he became conscious of a singular sort of grin upon every face. This grin made him turn rapidly round to look for its cause. It explained itself at once. At his very elbow was a lady whom his heart recognized, though her back was turned to him. She was dressed in a rich silk gown, pearl white, with flowers and sprigs embroidered; her beautiful white neck and arms were bare. She was sweeping up the room with the epilogue in her hand, learning it off by heart; at the other end of the room she turned, and now she shone full upon him.

It certainly was a dazzling creature. She had a head of beautiful form, perched like a bird upon a throat massive, yet shapely and smooth as a column of alabaster; a symmetrical brow; black eyes, full of fire and tenderness; a delicious mouth, with a hundred varying expressions, and that marvellous faculty of giving beauty alike to love or scorn, a sneer or a smile. But she had one feature more remarkable than all — her eyebrows, the actor's feature; they were jet black, strongly marked, and in repose were arched like a rainbow; but it was their extraordinary flexibility which made other faces upon the stage look sleepy beside Margaret Woffington's. In person she was considerably above the middle height, and so finely formed that one could not determine the exact character of her figure. At one time it seemed all stateliness, at another time elegance personified, and flowing voluptuousness at another: She was Juno, Psyche, Hebe, by turns, and for aught we know at will.

It must be confessed that a sort of halo of personal grandeur surrounds a great actress. A scene is set; half a dozen nobodies are there lost in it, because they are and seem lumps of nothing. The great artist steps upon that scene, and how she fills it in a moment! Mind and majesty wait upon her in the air; her person is lost in the greatness of her personal presence; she dilates with *thought,* and a stupid giantess looks a dwarf beside her.

No wonder, then, that Mr. Vane felt overpowered by this torch in a closet. To vary the metaphor, it seemed to him, as she swept up and down, as if the greenroom was a shell, and this glorious creature must burst it and be free. Meantime, the others saw a pretty actress studying her business; and Cibber saw a dramatic school girl, learning what he presumed to be a very silly set of words. Sir C. Pomander's eye had been on her the moment she entered, and he watched keenly the effect of Vane's eloquent eulogy; but apparently the actress was too deep in her epilogue for any thing else. She came in saying "Mum, mum, mum," over her task, and she went on doing so. The experienced Mr. Cibber, who had divined Vane in an instant, drew him into a corner, and complimented him on his well-timed eulogy.

"You acted that mighty well, sir," said he. "Stop my vitals, if I did not think you were in earnest, till I saw the jade had slipped in among us. It told, sir; it told."

Up fired Vane. "What do you mean, sir?" said he. "Do you suppose my admiration of that lady is feigned?"

"No need to speak so loud, sir," replied the

old gentleman; "she hears you. These hussies have ears like hawks."

He then dispensed a private wink and a public bow, with which he strolled away from Mr. Vane, and walked feebly and jantily up the room, whistling "Fair Hebe," fixing his eye upon the past, and somewhat ostentatiously overlooking the existence of the present company.

There is no great harm in an old gentleman whistling, but there are two ways of doing it; and as this old beau did it, it seemed not unlike a small cock-a-doodle-doo of general defiance; and the denizens of the greenroom, swelled now to a considerable number by the addition of all the ladies and gentlemen who had been killed in the fourth act, or whom the buttery-fingered author could not keep in hand until the fall of the curtain, felt it as such; and so they were not sorry when Mrs. Woffington, looking up from her epilogue, cast a glance upon the old beau, waited for him, and walked parallel with him on the other side the room, giving an absurdly exact imitation of his carriage and deportment. To make this more striking, she pulled out of her pocket, after a mock search, a huge paste ring, gazed on it with a ludicrous affectation of simple wonder, stuck it, like Cibber's diamond, on her little finger, and pursing up her mouth, proceeded to whistle a quick movement, —

> "Which by some devilish cantrip sleight,"

played round the old beau's slow movement without being at variance with it. As for the character of this ladylike performance, it was clear, brilliant, and loud as blacksmith.

The folks laughed; Vane was shocked. "She profanes herself by whistling," thought he. Mr. Cibber was confounded. He appeared to have no idea whence came this sparkling adagio. He looked round, placed his hands to his ears, and left off whistling. So did his musical accomplice.

"Gentlemen," said Cibber, with pathetic gravity, "the wind howls most dismally this evening! I took it for a drunken shoemaker!"

At this there was a roar of laughter, except from Mr. Vane. Peg Woffington laughed as merrily as the others, and showed a set of teeth that were really dazzling; but all in one moment, without the preliminaries an ordinary countenance requires, this laughing Venus pulled a face gloomy beyond conception. Down came her black brows, straight as a line, and she cast a look of bitter reproach on all present; resuming her study, as who should say, "Are ye not ashamed to divert a poor girl from her epilogue?" And then she went on, "Mum, mum, mum," casting off, ever and anon, resentful glances; and this made the fools laugh again.

The laureate was now respectfully addressed by one of his admirers, James Quin, the Falstaff of the day, and the rival at this time of Garrick in tragic characters, though the general opinion was, that he could not long maintain a stand against the younger genius and his rising school of art.

Off the stage James Quin was a character; his eccentricities were three; a humorist, a glutton, and an honest man — traits that often caused astonishment and ridicule, especially the last.

"May we not hope for something from Mr. Cibber's pen after so long a silence?"

"No," was the considerate reply. "Who have ye got to play it?"

"Plenty," said Quin; "there's your humble servant; there's ——"

"Humility at the head of the list," cried she of the epilogue. "Mum, mum, mum!"

Vane thought this so sharp!

"Garrick, Barry, Macklin, Kitty Clive here at my side, Mrs. Cibber, the best tragic actress I ever saw; and Woffington, who is as good a comedian as you ever saw, sir!" and Quin turned as red as fire.

"Keep your temper, Jemmy," said Mrs. Woffington, with a severe accent. "Mum, mum, mum!"

"You misunderstand my question," replied Cibber, calmly; "I know your *dramatis personæ*, but where the devil are your actors?"

Here was a blow.

"The public," said Quin, in some agitation, "would snore, if we acted as they did in your time."

"How do you know that, sir?" was the supercilious rejoinder; "*you never tried!*"

Mr. Quin was silenced. Peg Woffington looked off her epilogue.

"Bad as we are," said she, coolly, "we might be worse."

Mr. Cibber turned round, slightly raised his eyebrows,—

"Indeed!" said he. "Madam!" added he, with a courteous smile, "will you be kind enough to explain to me how you could be worse?"

"If, like a crab, we could go backwards!"

At this the auditors tittered; and Mr. Cibber had recourse to his spy-glass.

This gentleman was satirical or insolent, as the case might demand, in three degrees, of which the snuffbox was the comparative, and the spy-glass the superlative. He had learned this on the stage. In annihilating Quin he had just used the snuff weapon, and now he drew his spy-glass upon poor Peggy.

"Whom have we here?" said he; then he looked with his spy-glass to see. "O, the little Irish orange girl!"

"Whose basket outweighed Colly Cibber's salary for the first twenty years of his dramatic career," was the delicate reply to the above delicate remark. It staggered him for a moment;

however, he affected a most puzzled air, then gradually allowed a light to steal into his features.

"Eh! ah! O, how stupid I am! I understand; you sold something besides oranges!"

"O," said Mr. Vane, and colored up to the temples, and cast a look on Cibber, as much as to say, "If you were not seventy-three!"

His ejaculation was something so different from any tone any other person there present could have uttered, that the actress's eye dwelt on him for a single moment, and in that moment he felt himself looked through and through.

"I sold the young fops a bargain, you mean," was her calm reply; "and now I am come down to the old ones. A truce, Mr. Cibber. What do you understand by an actor? Tell me, for I am foolish enough to respect your opinion on these matters."

"An actor, young lady," said he, gravely, "is an artist who has gone deep enough in his art to make dunces, critics, and greenhorns take it for nature; moreover, he really personates; which your mere *man of the stage* never does. He has learned the true art of self-multiplication. He drops Betterton, Booth, Wilkes, or, a-hem ——"

"Cibber," inserted Sir Charles Pomander. Cibber bowed.

"In his dressing room, and comes out young or old, a fop, a valet, a lover, or a hero, with voice, mien, and every gesture to match. A grain less than this may be good speaking, fine preaching, deep grunting, high ranting, eloquent reciting; but I'll be hanged if it is acting!"

"Then Colly Cibber never acted," whispered Quin to Mrs. Clive.

"Then Margaret Woffington is an actress," said M. W. "The fine ladies take my Lady Betty for their sister. In Mrs. Day I pass for a woman of seventy; and in Sir Harry Wildair I have been taken for a man. I would have told you that before, but I didn't know it was to my credit," said she, slyly, "till Mr. Cibber laid down the law."

"Proof!" said Cibber.

"A warm letter from one lady, diamond buckles from another, and an offer of her hand and fortune from a third; *rien que cela.*"

Mr. Cibber conveyed behind her back a look of absolute incredulity; she divined it.

"I will not show you the letters," continued

she, "because Sir Harry, though a rake, was a gentleman; but here are the buckles;" and she fished them out of her pocket, capacious of such things. The buckles were gravely inspected; they made more than one eye water; they were undeniable.

"Well, let us see what we can do for her," said the laureate. He tapped his box, and without a moment's hesitation produced the most execrable distich in the language: —

"Now who is like Peggy, with talent at will,
A maid loved her Harry, *for want of a Bill?*"

"Well, child," continued he, after the applause which follows extemporary verses had subsided, "take *me* in. Play something to make me lose sight of saucy Peg Woffington, and I'll give the world five acts more before the curtain falls on Colly Cibber."

"If you could be deceived," put in Mr. Vane, somewhat timidly; "I think there is no disguise through which grace and beauty such as Mrs. Woffington's would not shine, to my eyes."

"That is to praise my person at the expense of my wit, sir, is it not?" was her reply.

This was the first word she had ever addressed to him; the tones appeared so sweet to him that he could not find any thing to reply for listening to them; and Cibber resumed: —

"Meantime, I will show you a real actress; she is coming here to-night to meet me. Did ever you children hear of Ann Bracegirdle?"

"Bracegirdle!" said Mrs. Clive; "why, she has been dead this thirty years; at least I thought so."

"Dead to the stage. There is more heat in her ashes than in your fire, Kate Clive! Ah, here comes her messenger," continued he, as an ancient man appeared, with a letter in his hand. This letter Mrs. Woffington snatched and read, and at the same instant in bounced the call boy. "Epilogue called," said this urchin, in the tone of command which these small fry of Parnassus adopt; and obedient to his high behest, Mrs. Woffington moved to the door with the Bracegirdle missive in her hand, but not before she had delivered its general contents. "The great actress will be here in a few minutes," said she, and she glided swiftly out of the room.

CHAPTER II.

People whose mind or manners possess any feature, and are not as devoid of all eccentricity as half pounds of butter bought of metropolitan grocers, are recommended not to leave a room full of their acquaintances until the last but one. Yes, they should always be penultimate. Perhaps Mrs. Woffington knew this; but epilogues are stubborn things, and call boys undeniable.

"Did you ever hear a woman whistle before?"

"Never; but I saw one sit astride on an ass in Germany."

"The saddle was not on her husband, I hope, madam!"

"No, sir; the husband walked by his kinsfolk's side, and made the best of a bad bargain, as Peggy's husband will have to."

"Wait till some one ventures on the gay Lotharia — *illi æs triplex*; that means he must have triple brass, Kitty."

"I deny that, sir, since his wife will always have enough for both."

"I have not observed the lady's brass," said Vane, trembling with passion; "but I observed her talent, and I noticed that whoever attacks her to her face comes badly off."

"Well said, sir," answered Quin; "and I wish Kitty here would tell us why she hates Mrs. Woffington, the best natured woman in the theatre."

"I don't hate her; I don't trouble my head about her."

"Yes, you hate her; for you never miss a cut at her, never."

"Do you hate a haunch of venison, Quin?" said the lady.

"No, you little unnatural monster!" replied Quin.

"For all that, you never miss a cut at one; so hold your tongue."

"*Le beau raisonnement!*" said Mr. Cibber. "James Quin, don't interfere with Nature's laws; let our ladies hate one another; it eases their minds. Try to make them Christians, and you will not convert their tempers, but spoil your own. Peggy, there, hates George Anne Bellamy because she has gaudy silk dresses from Paris, by paying for them, as *she* could, if not too stin gy. Kitty, here, hates Peggy because Rich has breeched her; whereas Kitty, who now sets up for a prude, wanted to put delicacy off, and small clothes on, in Peg's stead; that is where the Kate and Peg shoe pinches, near the femoral artery, James."

"Shrimps have the souls of shrimps," resumed this *censor castigatorque minorum.* "Listen to me, and learn that really great actors are great in soul, and do not blubber like a great school girl because Anne Bellamy has two yellow silk dresses from Paris, as I saw Woffington blubber in this room, and would not be comforted; nor fume like Kitty Clive, because Woffington has a pair of breeches and a little boy's rapier to go a playing at acting with. When I was young, two giantesses fought for empire upon this very stage, where now dwarfs crack and bounce like parched peas. They played Roxana and Statira in the 'Rival Queens.' Rival queens of art themselves, they put out all their strength. In the middle of the last act the town gave judgment in favor of Statira. What did Roxana? Did she spill grease on Statira's robe as Peg Woffington would? or stab her, as I believe Kitty, here, capable of doing? No! Statira was never so tenderly killed as that night: she owned this to me. Roxana bade the theatre farewell that night, and wrote to Statira thus — I give you word for word: 'Madam, the best judge we have has decided in your favor. I shall never play second on a stage where I have been first so long; but I shall often be a spectator, and methinks none will appreciate your talent more than I, who have felt its weight. My wardrobe, one of the best in Europe, is of no use to me; if you will honor me by selecting a few of my dresses, you will gratify me, and I shall fancy I see myself upon the stage to greater advantage than before.'"

"And what did Statira answer, sir?" said Mr. Vane, eagerly.

"She answered thus: 'Madam, the town has often been wrong, and may have been so last night, in supposing that I vied successfully with your merit; but thus much is certain, — and here, madam, I am the best judge, — that off the stage you have just conquered me. I shall wear with pride any dress you have honored, and shall feel inspired to great exertions by your presence among our spectators, unless, indeed, the sense of your magnanimity and the recollection of your talent should damp me by the dread of losing any portion of your good opinion.'"

"What a couple of stiff old things!" said Mrs. Clive.

"Nay, madam, say not so," cried Vane, warmly; "surely this was the lofty courtesy of two great minds not to be overbalanced by strife, defeat, or victory."

"What were their names, sir?"

"Statira was the great Mrs. Oldfield. Roxana you will see here to-night."

This caused a sensation.

Colly's reminiscences were interrupted by loud applause from the theatre; the present seldom gives the past a long hearing.

The old war horse cocked his ears.

"It is Woffington speaking the epilogue," said Quin.

"O, she has got the length of their foot somehow," said a small actress.

"And the breadth of their hands, too," said Pomander, waking from a nap.

"It is the depth of their hearts she has sounded," said Vane.

In those days, if a metaphor started up, the poor thing was coursed up hill and down dale, and torn limb from jacket; even in Parliament, a trope was sometimes hunted from one session into another.

"You were asking me about Mrs. Oldfield, sir," resumed Cibber, rather peevishly "I will own to you, I lack words to convey a just idea of her double and complete supremacy. But the comedians of this day are weak-strained *farceurs* compared with her, and her tragic tone was thunder set to music.

"I saw a brigadier general cry like a child at her Indiana. I have seen her crying with pain herself at the wing, (for she was always a great sufferer;) I have seen her then spring upon the stage as Lady Townley, and in a moment sorrow brightened into joy; the air seemed to fill with singing birds, that chirped the pleasures of fashion, love, and youth, in notes sparkling like diamonds, and stars, and prisms. She was above criticism, out of its scope, as is the blue sky; men went not to judge her; they drank her, and gazed at her, and were warmed at her, and refreshed by her. The fops were awed into silence, and with their humbler betters thanked Heaven for her, if they thanked it for any thing.

"In all the crowded theatre, care, and pain, and poverty were banished from the memory whilst Oldfield's face spoke, and her tongue flashed melodies; the lawyer forgot his quillets; the polemic the mote in his brother's eye; the old maid her grudge against the two sexes; the old man his gray hairs and his lost hours. And can it be that all this, which should have been immortal, is quite — quite lost, is as though it had never been?" he sighed. "Can it be that its fame is now sustained by me, who twang with my poor lute, cracked and old, these feeble praises of a broken lyre, —

"'Whose wires were golden, and its heavenly air
More tunable than lark to shepherd's ear,
When wheat is green, when hawthorn buds appear'?"

He paused, and his eye looked back over many years; then, with a very different tone, he added, —

"And that Jack Falstaff there must have seen her, now I think on't."

"Only once, sir," said Quin, "and I was but ten years old."

"He saw her once, and he was ten years old; yet he calls Woffington a great comedian, and my son The's wife, with her hatchet face, the greatest tragedian he ever saw! Jemmy, what an ass you must be!"

"Mrs. Cibber always makes me cry, and t'other always makes me laugh," said Quin, stoutly; "that's why."

Ce beau raisonnement met no answer but a look of sovereign contempt.

A very trifling incident saved the ladies of the British stage from further criticism. There were two candles in this room, one on each side; the call boy had entered, and poking about for something, knocked down and broke one of these.

"Awkward imp!" cried a velvet page.

"I'll go *to the Treasury* for another, ma'am," said the boy, pertly, and vanished with the fractured wax.

I take advantage of the interruption to open Mr. Vane's mind to the reader. First he had been astonished at the freedom of sarcasm these people indulged in without quarrelling; next at the non-respect of sex.

"So sex is not recognized in this community," thought he. Then the glibness and merit of some of their answers surprised and amused him. He, like me, had seldom met an imaginative repartee, except in a play or a book. "Society's" repartees were then, as they are now, the good old three in various dresses and veils: *Tu quoque, tu mentiris, vos damnemini;* but he was sick and dispirited, on the whole; such very bright illusions had been dimmed in these few minutes.

She was brilliant; but her manners, if not masculine, were very daring; and yet, when she spoke to him, a stranger, how sweet and gentle her voice was! Then it was clear nothing but his ignorance could have placed her at the summit of her art.

Still he clung to his enthusiasm for her. He drew Pomander aside. "What a simplicity there is in Mrs. Woffington!" said he; "the rest, male and female, are all so affected; she is so fresh and natural. They are all hothouse plants; she is a cowslip with the May dew on it."

"What you take for simplicity is her refined art," replied Sir Charles.

"No," said Vane, "I never saw a more innocent creature!"

Pomander laughed in his face. This laugh disconcerted him more than words; he spoke no more; he sat pensive. He was sorry he had come to this place, where every body knew his goddess; yet nobody admired, nobody loved, and alas! nobody respected her.

He was roused from his revery by a noise; the noise was caused by Cibber falling on Garrick, whom Pomander had maliciously quoted against all the tragedians of Colly Cibber's day.

"I tell you," cried the veteran, "that this Garrick has banished dignity from the stage, and given us in exchange what you and he take for fire; but it is smoke and vapor. His manner is little, like his person; it is all fuss and bustle. This is his idea of a tragic scene: A little fellow comes bustling in, goes bustling about, and runs bustling out." Here Mr. Cibber left the room, to give greater effect to his description, but presently returned in a mighty pother, saying, "'Give me another horse!' Well, where's the horse? Don't you see I'm waiting for him? 'Bind up my wounds!' Look sharp now with these wounds. 'Have mercy, Heaven!' but be quick about it, for the pit can't wait for Heaven. Bustle, bustle, bustle!"

The old dog was so irresistibly funny, that the whole company were obliged to laugh; but in the midst of their merriment Mrs. Woffington's voice was heard at the door.

"This way, madam."

A clear and somewhat shrill voice replied, "I know the way better than you, child," and a stately old lady appeared on the threshold.

"Bracegirdle," said Mr. Cibber.

It may well be supposed that every eye was turned on this new comer—that Roxana for whom Mr. Cibber's story had prepared a peculiar interest. She was dressed in a rich green velvet gown, with gold fringe. Cibber remembered it; she had played the "Eastern Queen" in it. Heaven forgive all concerned! It was fearfully pinched in at the waist and ribs, so as to give the idea of wood inside, not woman.

Her hair and eyebrows were iron gray, and she had lost a front tooth, or she would still have been eminently handsome. She was tall and straight as a dart, and her noble port betrayed none of the weakness of age, only it was to be seen that her hands were a little weak, and the gold-headed crutch struck the ground rather sharply, as if it did a little limbs'-duty.

Such was the lady who marched into the middle of the room, with a "How do, Colly?" and looking over the company's heads as if she did not see them, regarded the four walls with some interest. Like a cat, she seemed to think more of places than of folk. The page obsequiously offered her a chair.

"Not so clean as it used to be," said Mrs. Bracegirdle.

Unfortunately, in making this remark, the old lady graciously patted the page's head for offering her the chair; and this action gave, with some of the ill-constituted minds that are ever on the titter, a ridiculous direction to a remark intended, I believe, for the paint and wainscots, &c.

"Nothing is as it used to be," remarked Mr. Cibber.

"All the better for every thing," said Mrs. Clive.

"We were laughing at this mighty little David, first actor of this mighty little age."

Now, if Mr. Cibber thought to find in the new comer an ally of the past, in its indiscriminate attack upon the present, he was much mistaken; for the old actress made onslaught on this nonsense at once.

"Ay, ay," said she, "and not the first time by many hundreds. 'Tis a disease you have. Cure yourself, Colly. Davy Garrick pleases the public; and in trifles like acting, that take nobody to heaven, to please all the world is to be great. Some pretend to higher aims, but none have 'em. You may hide this from young fools, mayhap, but not from an old 'oman like me. He! he! he! No, no, no; not from an old 'oman like me."

She then turned round in her chair, and with that sudden, unaccountable snappishness of tone to which the brisk old are subject, she snarled, "Gie me a pinch of snuff, some of ye, do!"

Tobacco dust was instantly at her disposal. She took it with the points of her fingers, delicately, and divested the crime of half its uncleanness and vulgarity — more, an angel couldn't.

"Monstrous sensible woman, though!" whispered Quin to Clive.

"Hey, sir? what do you say, sir? for I'm a little deaf." (Not very to praise, it seems.)

"That your judgment, madam, is equal to the reputation of your talent."

The words were hardly spoken before the old lady rose upright as a tower. She then made an oblique preliminary sweep, and came down with such a courtesy as the young had never seen.

James Quin, not to disgrace his generation, attempted a corresponding bow, for which his figure and apoplectic tendency rendered him unfit; and whilst he was transacting it, the graceful Cibber stepped gravely up, and looked down and up the process with his glass, like a naturalist inspecting some strange capriccio of an orang-outang. The gymnastics of courtesy ended without backfalls — Cibber lowered his tone: —

"You are right, Bracy. It is nonsense deny ing the young fellow's talent; but his Othello, now, Bracy! be just — his Othello!"

"O dear! O dear!" cried she; "I thought it was Desdemona's little black boy come in without the tea kettle."

Quin laughed uproariously.

"It made me laugh a deal more than Mr. Quin's Falstaff. O dear! O dear!"

"Falstaff, indeed! Snuff!" in the tone of a trumpet.

Quin secretly revoked his good opinion of this woman's sense.

"Madam," said the page, timidly, "if you would but favor us with a specimen of the old style!"

"Well, child, why not? Only what makes you mumble like that? but they all do it now, I see. Bless my soul! our words used to come out like brandy cherries; but now a sentence is like raspberry jam, on the stage and off."

Cibber chuckled.

"And why don't you men carry yourselves like Cibber here?"

"Don't press that question," said Colly, dryly.

"A monstrous poor actor, though," said the merciless old woman, in a mock aside to the others; "only twenty shillings a week for half his life!" and her shoulders went up to her ears; then she fell into a half revery. "Yes, we were distinct," said she; "but I must own, children, we were slow. Once, in the midst of a beautiful tirade, my lover went to sleep, and fell against me. A mighty pretty epigram, twenty lines, was writ on't by one of my gallants. Have ye as many of them as we used?"

"In that respect," said the page, "we are not behind our great-grandmothers."

"I call that pert," said Mrs. Bracegirdle, with the air of one drawing scientific distinctions. "Now, is that a boy or a lady that spoke to me last?"

"By its dress, I should say a boy," said Cibber, with his glass; "by its assurance, a lady."

"There's one clever woman amongst ye; Peg something; plays Lothario, Lady Betty Modish, and what not."

"What! admire Woffington?" screamed Mrs. Clive. "Why, she is the greatest gabbler on the stage."

"I don't care," was the reply; "there's nature about the jade. Don't contradict me!" added she, with sudden fury; "a parcel of children!"

"No, madam," said Clive, humbly. "Mr. Cibber, will you try and prevail on Mrs. Bracegirdle to favor us with a recitation?"

Cibber handed his cane, with pomp, to a small actor. Bracegirdle did the same; and striking the attitudes that had passed for heroic in their day, they declaimed out of the "Rival Queens" two or three tirades, which I graciously spare the reader of this tale. Their elocution was neat and silvery; but not one bit like the way people speak in streets, palaces, fields, roads, and rooms. They had not made the grand discovery which Mr. A. Wigan on the stage, and every man of sense off it, has made in our day and nation — namely, that the stage is a representation not of stage, but of life; and that an actor ought to speak and act in imitation of human beings, not of speaking machines that have run and creaked in a stage groove, with their eyes shut upon the world at large, upon nature, upon truth, upon man, upon woman, and upon child.

"This is slow," cried Cibber; "let us show these young people how ladies and gentlemen moved fifty years ago, *dansons*."

A fiddler was caught, a beautiful slow minuet played, and a bit of "solemn dancing" done. Certainly it was not gay; but it must be owned it was beautiful: it was the dance of kings; the poetry of the courtly saloon.

The retired actress, however, had friskier notions left in her. "This is slow," cried she, and bade the fiddler play "The wind that shakes the barley"—an ancient jig tune. This she danced to in a style that utterly astounded the spectators.

She showed them what fun was: her feet and her stick were all echoes to the mad strain; out went her heel behind, and returning, drove her four yards forward. She made unaccountable slants, and cut them all over in turn if they did not jump for it. Roars of inextinguishable laughter arose; it would have made an oyster merry. Suddenly she stopped, and put her hands to her sides; and soon after she gave a vehement cry of pain.

The laughter ceased.

She gave another cry of such agony that they were all round her in a moment.

"O, help me, ladies!" screamed the poor woman, in tones as feminine as they were heart-rending and piteous. "O, my back! my loins! I suffer, gentlemen," said the poor thing, faintly.

What was to be done? Mr. Vane offered his penknife to cut her laces.

"You shall cut my head off sooner," cried she with sudden energy. "Don't pity me," said she, sadly, "I don't deserve it;" then lifting her eyes, she exclaimed, with a sad air of self-reproach, "O vanity! do you never leave a woman?"

"Nay, madam," whimpered the page, who was a good hearted girl; "'twas your great complaisance for us, not vanity. O, O, O!" and she began to blubber to make matters better.

"No, my children," said the old lady, "'twas vanity. I wanted to show you what an old 'oman could do, and I have humiliated myself, trying to outshine younger folk. I am justly humiliated, as you see;" and she began to cry a little.

"This is very painful," said Cibber.

Mrs. Bracegirdle now raised her eyes, (they had set her in a chair,) and looking sweetly, tenderly, and earnestly on her old companion, she said to him, slowly, gently, but impressively,—

"Colly, at threescore years and ten, this was ill done of us. You and I are here now—for what? to cheer the young up the hill we mounted years ago. And, old friend, if we detract from them we discourage them. A great sin in the old."

"Every dog his day."

"We have had ours." Here she smiled; then

laying her hand tenderly in the old man's, she added, with calm solemnity, "And now we must go quietly towards our rest, and strut and fret no more the few last minutes of life's fleeting hour."

How tame my cacotype of these words compared with what they were! I am ashamed of them and myself, and the human craft of writing, which, though commoner far, is so miserably behind the godlike art of speech. *Si ipsam audivisses!*

These ink scratches, which, in the imperfection of language we have called words, till the unthinking actually dream they are words, but which are the shadows of the corpses of words; these word-shadows then were living powers on her lips, and subdued, as eloquence always does, every heart within reach of the imperial tongue.

The young loved her, and the old man, softened and vanquished, and mindful of his failing life, was silent, and pressed his handkerchief to his eyes a moment; then he said,—

"No, Bracy; no! Be composed, I pray you. She is right. Young people, forgive me that I love the dead too well, and the days when I was what you are now. Drat the woman," continued he, half ashamed of his emotion; "she makes us laugh, and makes us cry, just as she used."

"What does he say, young woman?" said the old lady, dryly, to Mrs. Clive.

"He says you make us laugh, and make us cry, madam; and so you do me, I'm sure."

"And that's Peg Woffington's notion of an actress! Better it, Cibber and Bracegirdle, if you can," said the other, rising up like lightning.

She then threw Colly Cibber a note, and walked coolly and rapidly out of the room, without looking once behind her.

The rest stood transfixed, looking at one another, and at the empty chair. Then Cibber opened and read the note aloud. It was from Mrs. Bracegirdle: "Playing at tric-trac; so can't play the fool in your greenroom to night. — B."

On this a musical, ringing laugh was heard from outside the door, where the pseudo Bracegirdle was washing the gray from her hair, and the wrinkles from her face, — ah, I wish I could do it as easily, — and the little bit of sticking plaster from her front tooth.

"Why, it is the Irish jade!" roared Cibber.

"Divil a less!" rang back a rich brogue; "and it's not the furst time we put the comether upon ye, England, my jewal!"

One more mutual glance, and then the mortal cleverness of all this began to dawn on their minds; and they broke forth into clapping of hands, and gave this accomplished *mime* three rounds of applause; Mr. Vane and Sir Charles Pomander leading with "Brava, Woffington!"

Its effect on Mr. Vane may be imagined. Who but she could have done this? This was as if a painter should so paint a man as to deceive his species. This was acting, but not like the acting of the stage. He was in transports, and self-satisfaction at his own judgment mingled pleasantly with his admiration.

In this cheerful exhibition one joined not — Mr. Cibber. His theories had received a shock, and we all love our theories. He himself had received a rap, and we don't hate ourselves.

Great is the syllogism! But there is a class of arguments less vulnerable.

If A says to B, "You can't hit me, as I prove

by this syllogism," (here followeth the syllogism,) and B, *pour toute réponse*, knocks A down such a whack that he rebounds into a sitting posture; and to him the man, the tree, the lamp post, and the fire escape become not clearly distinguishable; this barbarous logic prevails against the logic in Barbara, and the syllogism is in the predicament of Humpty Dumpty.

In this predicament was the poet laureate. "The miscreant Proteus (could not) escape these chains!" So the miscreant Proteus — no bad name for an old actor — took his little cocked hat and marched, a smaller, if not a wiser man. Some disjointed words fell from him, "Mimicry is not acting," &c.; and with one bitter, mowing glance at the applauders, *circumferens acriter oculos*, he vanished in the largest pinch of snuff on record. The rest dispersed more slowly.

Mr. Vane waited eagerly, and watched the door for Mrs. Woffington; but she did not come. He then made acquaintance with good natured Mr. Quin, who took him upon the stage, and showed him by what vulgar appliances that majestic rise of the curtain he so much admired was effected. Returning to the greenroom for his friend, he found him in animated conversation with Mrs. Woffington. This made Vane uneasy.

Sir Charles, up to the present moment of the evening, had been unwontedly silent, and now he was talking nineteen to the dozen, and Mrs. Woffington was listening with an appearance of interest that sent a pang to poor Vane's heart; he begged Mr. Quin to introduce him.

Mr. Quin introduced him.

The lady received his advances with polite composure. Mr. Vane stammered his admiration of her Bracegirdle; but all he could find words to say was mere general praise, and somewhat coldly received. Sir Charles, on the contrary, spoke more like a critic. "Had you given us the stage cackle, or any of those traditionary symptoms of old age, we should have instantly detected you," said he; "but this was art copying nature, and it may be years before such a triumph of illusion is again effected under so many adverse circumstances."

"You are very good, Sir Charles," was the reply. "You flatter me. It was one of those things which look greater than they are; nobody here knew Bracegirdle but Mr. Cibber; Mr. Cibber cannot see well without his glasses, and I got rid of one of the candles ; I sent one of the imps of the theatre to knock it down. I know Mrs. Bracegirdle by heart. I drink tea with her every Sunday. I had her dress on, and I gave the old boy her words and her way of thinking ; it was mere mimicry ; it was nothing compared with what I once did ; but, ahem ! "

"Pray tell us ! "

"I am afraid I shall shock your friend. I see he is not a wicked man like you, and perhaps does not know what good-for-nothing creatures actresses are."

"He is not so ignorant as he looks," replied Sir Charles.

"That is not quite the answer I expected, Sir Charles," replied this lively lady ; "but it serves me right for fishing on dry land. Well, then, you must know, a young gentleman courted me. I forget whether I liked him or not ; but you will fancy I hated him, for I promised to marry him. You must understand, gentlemen, that I was sent into the world, not to act, which I abominate, but to chronicle small beer and teach an army of little brats their letters ; so this word 'wife,' and that word 'chimney corner,' took possession of my mind, and a vision of darning stockings for a large party, all my own, filled my heart, and really I felt quite grateful to the little brute that was to give me all this, and he would have had such a wife as men never do have, still less deserve. But one fine day that the theatre left me time to examine his manner towards me, I instantly discovered he was deceiving me. So I had him watched, and the little brute was going to marry another woman, and break it to me by degrees afterwards, &c. You know, Sir Charles? Ah, I see you do.

"I found her out; got an introduction to her father; went down to his house three days before the marriage, with a little coal-black mustache, regimentals, and what not, made up, in short, with the art of my sex, gentlemen, and the impudence of yours.

"The first day I flirted and danced with the bride. The second I made love to her, and at night I let her know that her intended was a villain. I showed her letters of his; protestations, oaths of eternal fidelity to one Peg Woffington, 'who will die,' drawled I, if he betrays her.

"And here, gentlemen, mark the justice of Heaven. I received a back-handed slap: 'Peg Woffington! an actress! O, the villain!' cried she; 'let him marry the little vagabond. How dare he insult me with his hand that had been offered in such a quarter!'

"So, in a fit of virtuous indignation, the little hypocrite dismissed the little brute; in other words, she had fallen in love with me.

"I have not had many happy hours, but I remember it was delicious to look out of my window, and at the same moment smell the honeysuckles and see my *perfide* dismissed under a heap of scorn and a pile of luggage he had brought down for his wedding tour.

"I scampered up to London, laughing all the way; and when I got home, if I remember right, I cried for two hours. How do you account for that?"

"I hope, madam," said Vane, gravely, "it was remorse for having trifled with that poor young lady's heart; she had never injured you."

"But, sir, the husband I robbed her of was a brute and a villain in his little way, and wicked, and good for nothing, &c. He would have deceived that poor little hypocrite, as he had this one," pointing to herself.

"That is not what I mean; you inspired her with an attachment, never to be forgotten. Poor lady; how many sleepless nights has she passed since then, how many times has she strained her eyes to see her angel lover returning to her! She will not forget in two years the love it cost you but two days to inspire. The powerful should be merciful. Ah! I fear you have no heart."

These words had no sooner burst from Mr. Vane, than he was conscious of the strange liberty he had taken, and, indeed, the bad taste he had been guilty of; and this feeling was not lessened when he saw Mrs. Woffington color up to the temples. Her eyes, too, glittered like basilisks; but she said nothing, which was remarkable in her, whose tongue was the sword of a *maître d'armes.*

Sir Charles eyed his friend in a sly, satirical manner; he then said, laughingly, "In two months *she married a third!* don't waste your sympathy," and turned the talk into another channel; and soon after, Mrs. Woffington's maid appearing at the door, she curtesied to both gentlemen, and left the theatre. Sir Charles Pomander accompanied Mr. Vane a little way.

"What becomes of her innocence?" was his first word.

"One loses sight of it in her immense talent," said the lover.

"She certainly is clever in all that bears upon her business," was the reply; "but I noticed you were a little shocked with her indelicacy in telling us that story, and still more in having it to tell."

"Indelicacy? No!" said Vane; "the little brute deserved it. Good heavens! to think that 'a little brute' might have married that angel, and actually broke faith to lose her; it is incredible; the crime is diluted by the absurdity."

"Have you heard him tell the story? No? Then take my word for it, you have not heard the facts of the case."

"Ah! you are prejudiced against her?"

"On the contrary, I like her. But I know that with all women, the present lover is an angel and the past a demon, and so on in turn. And I know that if Satan were to enter the women of the stage, with the wild idea of impairing their veracity, he would come out of their minds a greater liar than he went in, and the innocent darlings would never know their spiritual father had been at them."

Doubtful whether this sentiment and period could be improved, Sir Charles parted with his friend, leaving his sting in him like a friend; the other's reflections as he sauntered home were not strictly those of a wise, well-balanced mind; they ran in this style: —

"When she said, 'Is not that to praise my person at the expense of my wit?' I ought to have said, 'Nay, madam; could your wit disguise your person, it would betray itself; so you would still shine confessed;' and instead of that I said nothing!"

He then ran over in his mind all the opportunities he had had for putting in something smart, and bitterly regretted those lost opportunities; and made the smart things, and beat the air with them. Then his cheeks tingled when he remembered that he had almost scolded her; and he concocted a very different speech, and straightway repeated it in imagination.

This is lovers' pastime; I own it funny; but it is open to one objection: this single practice of sitting upon eggs no longer chickenable, carried to a habit, is capable of turning a solid intellect into a liquid one, and ruining a mind's career.

We leave Mr. Vane, therefore, with a hope that he will not do it every night; and we follow his friend to the close of our chapter.

Hey for a definition!

What is diplomacy? Is it folly in a coat that looks like sagacity? Had Sir Charles Pomander, instead of watching Mr. Vane and Mrs. Woffington, asked the former whether he admired the latter, and whether the latter responded, straightforward Vane would have told him the whole truth in a minute. Diplomacy therefore was, as it often is, a waste of time.

But diplomacy did more in this case; it *sapienter descendebat in fossam*; it fell on its nose with gymnastic dexterity, as it generally does, upon my word.

To watch Mrs. Woffington's face *vis-à-vis* Mr. Vane, Pomander introduced Vane to the green-room of the Theatre Royal, Covent Garden. By this Pomander learned nothing, because Mrs.

Woffington had, with a wonderful appearance of openness, the closest face in Europe when she chose.

On the other hand, by introducing this country gentleman to this greenroom, he gave a mighty impulse and opportunity to Vane's love ; an opportunity which he forgot the timid, inexperienced Damon might otherwise never have found.

Here diplomacy was not policy, for as my sagacious reader has perhaps divined, Sir Charles Pomander *was after her himself.*

CHAPTER III.

YES : Sir Charles was *after* Miss Woffington. I use that phrase because it is a fine generic one, suitable to different kinds of love-making.

Mr. Vane's sentiments were an inexplicable compound ; but respect, enthusiasm, and deep admiration were the uppermost.

The good Sir Charles was no enigma : he had a vacancy in his establishment — a very high situation, too, for those who like that sort of thing — the head of his table, his left hand when he drove in the Park, &c. To this he proposed to promote Miss Woffington. She was handsome and witty, and he liked her. But that was not what caused him to pursue her ; slow, sagacious, inevitable, as a beagle.

She was celebrated, and would confer great *éclat* on him. The scandal of possessing her was a burning temptation. Women admire celebrity in a man ; but men adore it in a woman.

> "The world says, Philip is a famous man;
> What will not women love so taught?"

I will try to answer this question.

The women will more readily forgive disgusting physical deformity for Fame's sake, than we. They would embrace with more rapture a famous orang-outang, than we an illustrious chimpanzee; but when it comes to moral deformity the tables are turned.

Had the queen pardoned Mr. Greenacre and Mrs. Manning, would the great rush have been on the hero, or the heroine? Why, on Mrs. Macbeth! To her would the blackguards have brought honorable proposals, and the gentry liberal ones.

Greenacre would have found more female admirers than I ever shall; but the grand stream of sexual admiration would have set Mariawards. This fact is as dark as night; but it is as sure as the sun.

The next day "the friends" (most laughable of human substantives!) met in the theatre, and again visited the greenroom; and this time Vane determined to do himself more justice. He was again disappointed: the actress's manner was ceremoniously polite. She was almost constantly on the stage, and in a hurry when off it; and when there was a word to be got with her, the ready, glib Sir Charles was sure to get it. Vane could not help thinking it hard that a man who professed no respect for her, should thus keep the light from him; and he could hardly conceal his satisfaction, when Pomander, at night, bade him farewell for a fortnight. Pressing business took Sir Charles into the country.

The good Sir Charles, however, could not go without leaving his sting behind as a companion to his friend. He called on Mr. Vane, and after a short preface, containing the words, "our friendship," "old kindness," "my greater experience," he gravely warned him against Mrs. Woffington.

"Not that I would say this if you could take her for what she is, and amuse yourself with her as she will with you, if she thinks it worth her while. But I see you have a heart, and she will make a football of it, and torment you beyond all you have ever conceived of human anguish."

Mr. Vane colored high, and was about to interrupt the speaker; but he continued, —

"There, I am in a hurry. But ask Quin, or any body who knows her history; you will find she has had scores of lovers, and no one remains her friend after they part."

"Men are such villains!"

"Very likely," was the reply; "but twenty men don't ill use one good woman: those are not the proportions. Adieu."

This last hit frightened Mr. Vane; he began to look into himself; he could not but feel that he was a mere child in this woman's hands; and more than that, his conscience told him that if his heart should be made a football of, it would only be a just and probable punishment. For there were particular reasons why he, of all men, had no business to look twice at any woman whose name was Woffington.

That night he avoided the greenroom, though he could not forego the play; but the next night he determined to stay at home altogether. Accordingly, at five o'clock, the astounded box keeper wore a visage of dismay — there was no shilling for him! and Mr. Vane's nightly shilling had assumed the sanctity of salary in his mind.

Mr. Vane strolled disconsolate; he strolled by the Thames, he strolled up and down the Strand; and finally, having often admired the wisdom of moths in their gradual approach to what is not good for them, he strolled into the greenroom, Covent Garden, and sat down. When there, he did not feel happy. Besides, she had always been cold to him, and had given no sign of desiring his acquaintance, still less of recognition.

Mr. Vane had often seen a weathercock at work; and he had heard a woman compared to it; but he had never realized the simplicity, beauty, and justice of the simile. He was therefore surprised, as well as thrilled, when Mrs. Woffington, so cool, ceremonious, and distant hitherto, walked up to him in the greenroom, with a face quite wreathed in smiles, and without preliminary, thanked him for all the beautiful flowers he had sent her.

"What, Mrs. Woffington — what, you recognize me?"

"Of course; and have been foolish enough to feel quite supported by the thought I had at least one friend in the house. But," said she, looking down, "now you must not be angry; here are some stones that have fallen somehow among the flowers; I am going to give you them back, because I value flowers so I cannot have them mixed with any thing else; but don't ask me for a flower back," added she, seeing the color mount on his face, "for I would not give one of them to you or any body."

Imagine the effect of this on a romantic disposition like Mr. Vane's.

He told her how glad he was that she could distinguish his features amidst the crowd of her admirers; he confessed he had been mortified when he found himself, as he thought, entirely a stranger to her.

She interrupted him.

"Do you know your friend, Sir Charles Pomander? No! I am almost sure you do; well, he is a man I do not like. He is deceitful; besides, he is a wicked man. There, to be plain with you, he was watching me all that night, the first time you came here; and because I saw he was watching me, I would not know who you were, nor any thing about you."

"But you looked as if you had never seen me before."

"Of course I did, when I had made up my mind to," said the actress, naïvely.

"Sir Charles has left London for a fortnight; so if he is the only obstacle, I hope you will know me every night."

"Why, you sent me no flowers yesterday, or to-day."

"But I will to-morrow."

"Then I am sure I shall know your face again: good by. Won't you see me in the last act, and tell me how ill I do it?"

"O, yes!" and he hurried to his box; and so the actress secured one pair of hands for her last act.

He returned to the greenroom, but she did not revisit that verdant bower. The next night, after the usual compliments, she said to him, looking down with a sweet, engaging air, —

"I sent a messenger into the country to know about that lady."

"What lady?" said Vane, scarcely believing his senses.

"That you were so unkind to me about."

"I, unkind to you? what a brute I must be!"

"My meaning is, you justly rebuked me, only

you should not tell an actress she has no heart — that is always understood. Well, Sir Charles Pomander said she married a third in two months!"

"And did she?"

"No, it was in six weeks; that man never tells the truth, and since then she has married a fourth."

"I am glad of it!"

"So am I, since you awakened my conscience."

Delicious flattery! and of all flattery the sweetest, when a sweet creature does flattery, not merely utters it.

After this Vane made no more struggles. He surrendered himself to the charming seduction, and as his advances were respectful, but ardent and incessant, he found himself at the end of a fortnight Mrs. Woffington's professed lover.

They wrote letters to each other every day. On Sunday they went to church together in the morning, and spent the afternoon in the suburbs wherever grass was and dust was not.

In the next fortnight, poor Vane thought he had pretty well fathomed this extraordinary woman's character. Plumb the Atlantic with an eighty fathom line, sir!

"She is religious," said he; "she loves a church much better than a playhouse, and she never laughs nor goes to sleep in church, as I do. And she is breaking me of swearing — by degrees. She says that no fashion can justify what is profane, and that it must be vulgar as well as wicked. And she is frankness and simplicity itself."

Another thing that charmed him was her dis interestedness. She ordered him to buy her a present every day, but it was never to cost above a shilling. If an article could be found that cost exactly ten pence, (a favorite sum of hers,) she was particularly pleased; and these shilling presents were received with a flush of pleasure and brightening eyes; but when one day he appeared with a diamond necklace, it was taken very coldly; he was not even thanked for it; and he was made to feel, once for all, that the tenpenny ones were the best investments towards her favor.

Then he found out that she was very prudent and rather stingy; of Spartan simplicity in her diet, and a scorner of dress off the stage. To redeem this she was charitable, and her charity and her economy sometimes had a sore fight, during which she was peevish, poor little soul.

One day she made him a request.

"I can't bear you should think me worse than I am, and I don't want you to think me better than I am."

Vane trembled.

"But don't speak to others about me. Promise, and I will promise to tell you my whole story, whenever you are entitled to such a confidence."

"When shall I be entitled to it?"

"When I am sure you love me."

"Do you doubt that now?"

"Yes! I think you love me, but I am not sure."

"Margaret, remember I have known you much longer than you have known me."

"No!"

"Yes! Two months before we ever spoke I lived upon your face and voice."

"That is to say, you looked from your box at me upon the stage; and did not I look from the stage at you?"

"Never! You always looked at the pit, and my heart used to sink."

"On the 17th of May you first came into that box. I noticed you a little, the next day I noticed you a little more; I saw you fancied you liked me; after a while I could not have played without you."

Here was delicious flattery again, and poor Vane believed every word of it.

As for her request and her promise, she showed her wisdom in both these. As Sir Charles observed, it is a wonderful point gained if you allow a woman to tell her story her own way.

How the few facts that are allowed to remain, get moulded and twisted out of ugly forms into pretty shapes by those supple, dexterous fingers!

This present story cannot give the life of Mrs. Woffington, but only one great passage therein, as do the epic and dramatic writers; but since there was often great point in any sentences spoken on important occasions by this lady, I will just quote her defence of herself. The reader may be sure she did not play her weakest card; let us give her the benefit.

One day she and Kitty Clive were at it ding-dong; the greenroom was full of actors, male and female, but there were no strangers, and the ladies were saying things which the men of this generation only think ; at last Mrs. Woffington, finding herself roughly, and, as she thought, unjustly handled, turned upon the assembly and said, "What man did ever I ruin in all my life? Speak who can."

And there was a dead silence.

"What woman is there here at as much as three pounds per week even, that hasn't ruined two at the very least."

Report says there was a dead silence again, until Mrs. Clive perked up, and said she had only ruined one, and that was his own fault!

Mrs. Woffington declined to attach weight to this example. "Kitty Clive is the hook without the bait," said she ; and the laugh turned, as it always did, against Peggy's antagonist.

Thus much was speedily shown to Mr. Vane, that whatever were Mrs. Woffington's intentions towards him, interest had at present nothing to do with them ; indeed, it was made clear that even were she to surrender her liberty to him, it would only be as a princess, forging golden chains for herself with her own royal hand.

Another fortnight passed to the mutual satisfaction of the lovers. To Vane it was a dream of rapture to be near this great creature, whom thousands admired at such a distance; to watch over her, to take her to the theatre in a warm shawl, to stand at the wing and receive her as she came radiant from her dressing room, to watch her from her rear as she stood like some power about to descend on the stage, to see her falcon-like stoop upon the said stage, and hear the burst of applause that followed, as the report does the flash; to compare this with the spiritless crawl with which common artists went on, tame from their first note to their last; to take her hand when she came off, feel how her nerves were strung, like a greyhound's after a race, and her whole frame in a high, even glow, with the great Pythoness excitement of art.

And to have the same great creature leaning her head on his shoulder, and listening with a charming complacency, whilst he purred to her of love and calm delights, alternate with still greater triumphs; for he was to turn dramatic writer, for her sake was to write plays, a woman the hero, and love was to inspire him, and passion supply the want of pencraft. (You make me laugh, Mr. Vane!)

All this was heavenly.

And then with all her dash, and fire, and bravado, she was a thorough woman.

"Margaret!"

"Ernest!"

"I want to ask you a question. Did you really cry because that Miss Bellamy had dresses from Paris?"

"It does not seem very likely."

"No; but tell me, did you?"

"Who said I did?"

"Mr. Cibber."

"Old fool!"

"Yes; but did you?"

"Did I what?"

"Cry."

"Ernest, the minx's dresses were beautiful."

"No doubt; but did you cry?"

"And mine were dirty; I don't care about gilt rags, but dirty dresses, ugh!"

"Tell me, then."

"Tell you what?"

"Did you cry or not?"

"Ah, he wants to find out whether I am a fool, and despise me."

"No; I think I should love you better; for

hitherto I have seen no weakness in you, and it makes me uncomfortable."

"Be comforted! Is it not a weakness to like you?"

"You are free from that weakness, or you would gratify my curiosity."

"Be pleased to state, in plain, intelligible English, what you require of me."

"I want to know, in one word, did you cry or not?"

"Promise to tease me no more, then, and I'll tell you."

"I promise."

"You won't despise me?"

"Despise you? Of course not."

"Well, then — I don't remember!"

On another occasion, they were seated in the dusk, by the side of the canal in the Park, when a little animal began to potter about on an adjacent bank.

Mrs. Woffington contemplated it with curiosity and delight.

"O, you pretty creature!" said she. "Now you are a rabbit; at least, I think so."

"No," said Vane, innocently; "that is a rat."

"Ah, ah, ah!" screamed Mrs. Woffington, and pinched his arm. This frightened the rat, who disappeared. She burst out laughing, "There's a fool! The thing did not frighten me, and the name did. Depend upon it, it's true what they say, that off the stage I am the greatest fool there is. I'll never be so absurd again. Ah, ah, ah! here it is again!" (scream and pinch, as before.) "Do take me from this horrid place, where monsters come from the great deep."

And she flounced away, looking daggers askant at the place the rat had vacated in equal terror.

All this was silly, but it pleases us men; and contrast is so charming! This same fool was brimful of talent — and cunning, too, for that matter.

She played late that night, and Mr. Vane saw the same creature, who dared not stay where she was liable to a distant rat, spring upon the stage as a gay rake, and flash out her rapier, and act valor's king to the life, and seem ready to eat up every body, King Fear included; and then, after her brilliant sally upon the public, Sir Harry Wildair came and stood beside Mr. Vane.

Her bright skin, contrasted with her powdered periwig, became dazzling. She used little rouge, but that little made her eyes two balls of black lightning. From her high instep to her polished forehead all was symmetry. Her leg would have been a sculptor's glory; and the curve from her waist to her knee was Hogarth's line itself.

She stood like Mercury new lighted on a heaven-kissing hill. She placed her foot upon the ground as she might put a hand upon her lover's shoulder. We indent it with our eleven undisguised stone.

Such was Sir Harry Wildair, who stood by Mr. Vane, glittering with diamond buckles, gorgeous with rich satin breeches, velvet coat, ruffles, *pictai vestis et auri ;* and as she bent her long eye fringes down on him, (he was seated,) all her fiery charms gradually softened and quivered down to womanhood.

"The first time I was here," said Vane, "my admiration of you broke out to Mr. Cibber; and what do you think he said?"

"That you praised me for me to hear you. Did you?"

"Acquit me of such meanness."

"Forgive me. It is just what I should have done, had I been courting an actress."

"I think you have not met many ingenuous spirits, dear friend."

"Not one, my child."

This was a phrase she often applied to him now.

"The old fellow pretended to hear what I said, too; and I am sure you did not; did you?"

"Guess."

"I guess not."

"I am afraid I must plead guilty. An actress's ears are so quick to hear praise, to tell you the truth, I did catch a word or two, and 'it told, sir, it told.'"

"You alarm me! At this rate, I shall never know what you see, hear, or think, by your face."

"When you want to know any thing, ask me, and I will tell you; but nobody else shall learn any thing, nor even you, any other way."

"Did you hear the feeble tribute of praise I was paying you when you came in?" inquired Vane.

"No. You did not say that my voice had the compass and variety of nature, and my movements were free and beautiful, whilst the others when in motion were stilts, and coffee pots when in repose, did you?"

"Something of the sort, I believe," cried Vane, laughing.

"I melted from one fine statue into another, I restored the Antinous to his true sex. Goose! — Painters might learn their art from me, (in my dressing room, no doubt,) and orators revive at my lips the music of Athens, that quelled mad mobs and princes drunk with victory. Silly fellow! — Praise was never so sweet to me," murmured she, inclining like a goddess of love towards him; and he fastened on two velvet lips, that did not shun the sweet attack, but gently parted with a heavenly sigh, while her heaving bosom, and yielding frame, and swimming eyes confessed her conqueror.

That morning Mr. Vane had been dispirited, and apparently self-discontented; but at night he went home in a state of mental intoxication. His poetic enthusiasm, his love, his vanity, were all gratified at once. And all these, singly, have conquered Prudence and Virtue a million times.

She had confessed to him that she was disposed to risk her happiness on him; she had begged him to submit to a short probation; and she had promised, if her confidence and esteem remained unimpaired at the close of that period, — which was not to be an unhappy one, — to take advantage of the summer holidays, and cross the water with him, and forget every thing in the world with him, but love.

How was it that the very next morning, clouds chased one another across his face? Was it that men are happy but while the chase is doubtful? Was it the letter from Pomander announcing his return, and sneeringly inquiring whether he was still the dupe of Peg Woffington? or was it that same mysterious disquiet which attacked him periodically, and then gave way for a while to pleasure and her golden dreams?

The next day was to be a day of delight. He was to entertain her at his own house; and to do her honor, he had asked Mr. Cibber, Mr. Quin, and other actors, critics, &c.

Our friend Sir Charles Pomander had been

guilty of two ingenuities: first, he had written three or four letters, full of respectful admiration, to Mrs. Woffington, of whom he spoke slightingly to Vane; second, he had made a disingenuous purchase.

This purchase was Pompey, Mrs Woffington's little black slave. It is a horrid fact, but Pompey did not love his mistress: he was a little enamoured of her, as small boys are apt to be, but on the whole, a sentiment of hatred slightly predominated in his little black bosom.

It was not without excuse.

This lady was subject to two unpleasant companions, sorrow and bitterness. About twice a week she would cry for two hours; and after this class of fit she generally went abroad, and made a round of certain poor or sick *protégés* she had, and returned smiling and cheerful.

But other twice a week she might be seen to sit upon her chair, contracted into half her size, and looking daggers at the universe in general, the world in particular; and on these occasions, it must be owned, she staid at home, and sometimes whipped Pompey.

Pompey had not the sense to reflect that he

ought to have been whipped every day, nor the *esprit de corps* to be consoled by observing that this sort of thing did his mistress good. What he felt was, that his mistress, who did every thing well, whipped him with energy and skill; it did not take ten seconds, but still, in that brief period, Pompey found himself dusted and polished off.

The sacred principle of justice was as strong in Mrs. Woffington as in the rest of her sex; she had not one grain of it. When she was not in her tantrums, the mischievous imp was as sacred from check or remonstrance as a monkey, or a lapdog; and several female servants left the house on his account.

But Nemesis overtook him in the way we have hinted, and it put his little black pipe out.

The lady had taken him out of great humanity; he was fed like a game-cock, and dressed like a Barbaric prince; and once, when he was ill, his mistress watched him, and nursed him, and tended him with the same white hand that plied the obnoxious whip; and when he died, she alone withheld her consent from his burial, and this gave him a chance black boys never get, and he came to again; but still these tarnation lickings "stuck in him gizzard." So when Sir Charles's agent proposed to him certain silver coins, cheap at a little treachery, the ebony ape grinned till he turned half ivory, and became a spy in the house of his mistress.

The reader will have gathered, that the good Sir Charles had been quietly in London some hours before he announced himself as *paulo post futurum.*

Diamond cut diamond; a diplomate stole this march upon an actress, and took her black pawn. One for Pomander! (Gun.)

CHAPTER IV.

Triplet, the Cerberus of art, who had the first bark in this legend, and has since been out of hearing, ran from Lambeth to Covent Garden, on receipt of Mr. Vane's note. But ran he never so quick, he had built a full-sized castle in the air before he reached Bow Street.

The letter hinted at an order upon his muse for amatory verse : delightful task, cheering prospect.

Bid a man whose usual lot it is to break stones for the parish at ten pence the cubic yard; bid such a one play at marbles with stone taws for half an hour per day, and pocket one pound one. Bid a poor horse who has drawn those stones about, and browsed short grass by the wayside, bid him canter a few times round a grassy ring, and then go to his corn. In short, bid Rosinante change with Pegasus, and you do no more than Mr. Vane's letter held out to Triplet.

The amatory verse of that day was not up-hill work. There was a beaten track on a dead level, and you followed it. You told the tender creature, with a world of circumlocution, that, "without joking now," she was a leper, ditto a tigress, item marble. You next feigned a lucid interval, and to be on the point of detesting your monster; but in twenty more verses love became, as usual, stronger than reason, and you wound up your rotten yarn thus: —

You hugged a golden chain. You drew deeper into your wound a barbed shaft, like — (any wild animal will do, no one of them is such an ass, so you had an equal title to all;) and on looking back you saw with horrible complacency that you had inflicted one hundred locusts, five feet long, upon oppressed humanity.

Wont to travel over acres of canvas for a few shillings, and roods of paper on bare speculation, Triplet knew he could make a thousand a year at the above work without thinking.

He came, therefore, to the box keeper with his eyes glittering.

"Mr. Vane?"

"Just gone out with a gentleman."

"I'll wait, then."

Now Mr. Vane, we know, was in the greenroom, and went home by the stage door. The last thing he thought of was poor Triplet; the rich do not dream how they disappoint the poor. Triplet's castle fell as many a predecessor had. When the lights were put out, he left the theatre with a bitter sigh.

"If this gentleman knew how many sweet children I have, and what a good, patient, suffering wife, sure he would not have chosen me to make a fool of!" said the poor fellow to himself.

In Bow Street, he turned, and looked back upon the theatre. How gloomy and grand it loomed!

"Ah!" thought he, "if I could but conquer you; and why not? All history shows that nothing is unconquerable except perseverance. Hannibal conquered the Alps, and I'll conquer you," cried Triplet, firmly. "Yes, this visit is not lost; here I register a vow: I will force my way into that mountain of masonry, or perish in the attempt."

Triplet's most unpremeditated thoughts and actions often savored ridiculously of the sublime. Then and there, gazing with folded arms on this fortress of Thespis, the polytechnic man organized his first assault. The next evening he made it.

Five months previously he had sent the manager three great, large tragedies. He knew the aversion a theatrical manager has to read a manuscript play, not recommended by influential folk; an aversion which always has been carried to superstition. So he hit on the following scheme: —

He wrote Mr. Rich a letter; in this, he told Mr. Rich, that he (Triplet) was aware what a quantity of trash is offered every week to a manager, how disheartening it must be to read it all, and how natural, after a while, to read none. Therefore, he (Triplet) had provided that Mr. Rich might economize his time, and yet not remain in ignorance of the dramatic treasure that lay ready to his hand.

"The soul of a play," continued Triplet, "is the plot or fable. A gentleman of your experience can decide at once whether a plot or story is one to take the public!"

So then he drew out, in full, the three plots. He wrote these plots in verse! Heaven forgive us all, he really did. There were also two margins left; on one, which was narrow, he jotted down the *locale* per page of the most brilliant passages; on the other margin, which was as wide as the column of the plot, he made careful drawings of the personages in the principal dramatic situations; scrolls issued from their mouths, on which were written the words of fire that were flowing from each in these eruptions of the dramatic action. All was referred to pages in the manuscripts.

"By this means, sir," resumed the letter, "you will gut my fish in a jiffy; permit me to recall that expression, with apologies for my freedom. I would say, you will, in a few minutes of your valuable existence, skim the cream of Triplet."

This author's respect for the manager's time carried him into further and unusual details.

"Breakfast," said he, "is a quiet meal. Let me respectfully suggest, that by placing one of my plots on the table, with, say the sugar basin upon it, (this, again, is a mere suggestion,) and the play it appertains to on your other side, you can readily judge my work without disturbing the avocations of the day, and master a play in the twinkling of a teacup; forgive my facetiousness. This day month, at ten of the clock, I shall expect," said Triplet, with sudden severity, "sir, your decision!"

Then gliding back to the courtier, he formally disowned all special title to the consideration he expected from Mr. Rich's well-known courtesy; still, he begged permission to remind that gentleman, that he had six years ago painted for him a large scene, illuminated by two great poetical incidents: a red sun, of dimensions never seen out of doors in this or any country; and an ocean of sand, yellower than up to that time had been attained in art or nature; and that once, when the audience, late in the evening, had suddenly demanded a popular song from Mr. Nokes, he (Triplet) seeing the orchestra thinned by desertion, and nugatory by intoxication, had started from the pit, resuscitated with the whole contents of his snuffbox, the bass fiddle, snatched the leader's violin, and carried Mr. Nokes triumphantly through; that thunders of applause had followed, and Mr. Nokes had kindly returned thanks *for both;* but that he (Triplet) had hastily retired to evade the manager's acknowledgments, preferring to wait an opportunity like the present, when both interests could be conciliated, &c.

This letter he posted at its destination, to save time, and returned triumphant home. He had now forgiven and almost forgotten Vane; and had reflected that, after all, the drama was his proper walk.

"My dear," said he to Mrs. Triplet, "this family is on the eve of a great triumph!" Then, inverting that order of the grandiloquent and the homely which he invented in our first chapter, he proceeded to say, "I have reared in a single day a new avenue, by which histrionic greatness, hitherto obstructed, may become accessible. Wife, I think I have done the trick at last. Lysimachus!" added he, "let a libation be poured out on so smiling an occasion, and a burnt-offering rise to propitiate the celestial powers. Run to the 'Sun,' you dog. Three pennyworth of ale, and a hap'orth o' tobacco."

Ere the month was out, I am sorry to say, the Triplets were reduced to a state of beggary. Mrs. Triplet's health had long been failing; and although her duties at her little theatre were light and occasional, the manager was obliged to discharge her, since she could not be depended upon.

The family had not enough to eat! Think of that! They were not warm at night, and they felt gnawing and faintness often by day. Think of that!

Fortune was unjust here. The man was laughable, and a goose; and had no genius either for writing, painting, or acting; but in that he resembled most writers, painters, and actors of his own day and ours. He was not beneath the average of what men call art, and it is art's antipodes — treadmill artifice.

Other fluent ninnies shared gain, and even fame, and were called "pen-men," in Triplet's day. Other ranters were quietly getting rich by noise. Other liars and humbugs were painting out o' doors in-doors, and eating mutton instead of thistles for drenched stinging nettles, yclept trees; for block-tin clouds; for butler's pantry seas, and garret-conceived lakes; for molten sugar candy rivers; for airless atmosphere and sunless air; for carpet nature, and cold, dead fragments of an earth all soul and living glory to every cultivated eye but a routine painter's. Yet the man of many such mediocrities could not keep the pot boiling. We suspect

9

that to those who would rise in life, even strong versatility is a very doubtful good, and weak versatility ruination.

At last, the bitter, weary month was gone, and Triplet's eye brightened gloriously. He donned his best suit; and whilst tying his cravat, lectured his family. First, he complimented them upon their deportment in adversity; hinted that moralists, not experience, had informed him prosperity was far more trying to the character; put them all solemnly on their guard down to Lucy, ætat five, that they were *morituri* and *æ*, and must be pleased to abstain from "insolent gladness" upon his return.

"Sweet are the uses of adversity!" continued this cheerful monitor. "If we had not been hard up this while, we should not come with a full relish to meat three times a week, which, unless I am an ass, (and I don't see myself in that light,)" said Triplet, dryly, "will, I apprehend, be, after this day, the primary condition of our future existence."

"James, take the picture with you," said Mrs. Triplet, in one of those calm, little, desponding voices that fall upon the soul so agreeably when one is cock-a-hoop, and desires, with permission, so to remain.

"What on earth am I to take Mrs. Woffington's portrait for?"

"We have nothing in the house," said the wife, blushing.

Triplet's eye glittered like a rattlesnake's.

"The intimation is eccentric," said he. "Are you mad, Jane? Pray," continued he, veiling his wrath in scornful words, "is it requisite, heroic, or judicious, on the eve, or, more correctly, the morn, of affluence, to deposit an unfinished work of art with a mercenary relation. Hang it, Jane! would you really have me pawn Mrs. Woffington to-day?"

"James," said Jane, steadily, "the manager may disappoint you; we have often been disappointed; so take the picture with you. They will give you ten shillings on it."

Triplet was of those who see things roseate, Mrs. Triplet lurid.

"Madam," said the poet, "for the first time in our conjugal career, your commands deviate so entirely from reason, that I respectfully withdraw that implicit obedience which has hitherto constituted my principal reputation. I'm hanged if I do it, Jane!"

"Dear James, to oblige me!"

"That alters the case; you confess it is unreasonable?"

"O, yes! It is only to oblige me."

"Enough!" said Triplet, whose tongue was often a flail that fell on friend, foe, and self indiscriminately. "Allow it to be unreasonable, and I do it as a matter of course — to please you, Jane."

Accordingly the good soul wrapped it in green baize; but to relieve his mind he was obliged to get behind his wife, and shrug his shoulders to Lysimachus and the eldest girl, as who should say, *voilà bien une femme votre mère à vous!*

At last he was off in high spirits. He reached Covent Garden at half past ten, and there the poor fellow was sucked into our narrative whirlpool.

We must, however, leave him for a few minutes.

CHAPTER V.

Sir Charles Pomander was detained in the country much longer than he expected.

He was rewarded by a little adventure. As he cantered up to London with two servants and a postboy, all riding on horses ordered in relays beforehand, he came up with an antediluvian coach, stuck fast by the roadside. Looking into the window, with the humane design of quizzing the elders who should be there, he saw a young lady of surpassing beauty. This altered the case; Sir Charles instantly drew bridle and offered his services.

The lady thanked him; and being an innocent country lady, she opened those sluices, her eyes, and two tears gently trickled down, while she told him how eager she was to reach London, and how mortified at this delay.

The good Sir Charles was touched. He leaped his horse over a hedge, galloped to a farm house in sight, and returned with ropes and rustics.

These and Sir Charles's horses soon drew the coach out of some stiffish clay.

The lady thanked him, and thanked him, and thanked him, with heightening color and beaming eyes, and he rode away like a hero.

Before he had gone five miles, he became thoughtful and self-dissatisfied; finally, his remorse came to a head; he called to him the keenest of his servants, Hunsdon, and ordered him to ride back past the carriage; then follow, and put up at the same inn, to learn who the lady was, and whither going; and this knowledge gained, to ride into town full speed, and tell his master all about it. Sir Charles then resumed his complacency, and cantered into London that same evening.

Arrived there, he set himself in earnest to cut out his friend with Mrs. Woffington. He had already caused his correspondence with that lady to grow warm and more tender by degrees. Keeping a copy of his last, he always knew where he was. Cupid's barometer rose by rule; and so he arrived by just gradations at an artful climax, and made her, in terms of chivalrous affection, an offer of a house, &c., three hundred a year, &c., not forgetting his heart, &c. He knew that the ladies of the stage have an ear for flattery, and an eye to the main chance.

The good Sir Charles felt sure, that, however she might flirt with Vane or others, she would not forego a position for any disinterested *penchant.* Still, as he was a close player, he determined to throw a little cold water on that flame. His plan, like every thing truly scientific, was simple.

"I'll run her down to him, and ridicule him to her," resolved this faithful friend and lover dear.

He began with Vane. He found him just leaving his own house. After the usual compliments, some such dialogue as this took place between Telemachus and pseudo-Mentor: —

"I trust you are not really in the power of this actress."

"You are the slave of a word," replied Vane. "Would you confound black and white because both are colors? She is like that sisterhood in nothing but a name. Even on the stage they have nothing in common. They are puppets — all attitude and trick; she is all ease, grace, and nature."

"Nature!" cried Pomander. "*Laissez-moi tranquille.* They have artifice — nature's libel; she has art — nature's counterfeit."

"Her voice is truth told by music," cried the poetical lover; "theirs are jingling instruments of falsehood."

"They are all instruments," said the satirist; "she is rather the best tuned and played."

"Her face speaks in every lineament; theirs are rouged and wrinkled masks."

"Her mask is the best made, mounted, and moved; that is all."

"She is a fountain of true feeling."

"No; a pipe that conveys it without spilling or holding a drop."

"She is an angel of talent, sir."

"She's a devil of deception."

"She is a divinity to worship."

"She's a woman to fight shy of. There is not a woman in London better known," continued Sir Charles. "She is a fair actress on the boards, and a great actress off them; but I can tell you how to add a new charm to her."

"Heaven can only do that," said Vane, hastily.

"Yes, you can. Make her blush. Ask her for the list of your predecessors."

Vane winced visibly. He quickened his step as if to get rid of this gadfly.

"I spoke to Mr. Quin," said he, at last; "and he, who has no prejudice, paid her character the highest compliment."

"You have paid it the highest it admits," was the reply. "You have let it deceive you." Sir Charles continued in a more solemn tone, "Pray be warned. Why is it every man of intellect loves an actress once in his life, and no man of sense ever did it twice?"

This last hit, coming after the carte and tierce we have described, brought an expression of pain to Mr. Vane's face. He said, abruptly, "Excuse me, I desire to be alone for half an hour."

Machiavel bowed, and instead of taking offence, said, in a tone full of feeling, "Ah, I give you pain! But you are right; think it calmly over a while, and you will see I advise you well."

He then made for the theatre, and the weakish personage he had been playing upon walked down to the river, almost ran, in fact. He wanted to be out of sight.

He got behind some houses, and then his face seemed literally to break loose from confinement, so anxious, sad, fearful, and bitter were the expressions that coursed each other over that handsome countenance.

What is the meaning of these hot and cold fits? It is not Sir Charles who has the power to shake Mr. Vane so without some help from within. *There is something wrong about this man!*

CHAPTER VI.

Machiavel entered the greenroom, intending to wait for Mrs. Woffington, and carry out the second part of his plan.

He knew that weak minds cannot make head against ridicule, and with this pickaxe he proposed to clear the way before he came to grave, sensible, business love with the lady. Machiavel was a man of talent. If he has been a silent personage hitherto, it is merely because it was not his cue to talk, but listen ; otherwise, he was rather a master of the art of speech. He could be insinuating, eloquent, sensible, or satirical, at will. This personage sat in the greenroom. In one hand was his diamond snuffbox, in the other a richly laced handkerchief ; his clouded cane reposed by his side.

There was an air of success about this personage. The gentle reader, however conceited a dog, could not see how he was to defeat Sir Charles, who was tall, stout, handsome, rich, witty, self-sufficient, cool, majestic, courageous, and in whom were united the advantages of a hard head, a tough stomach, and no heart at all.

This great creature sat expecting Mrs. Woffington, like Olympian Jove awaiting Juno. But he was mortal after all; for suddenly the serenity of that adamantine countenance was disturbed; his eye dilated; his grace and dignity were shaken He huddled his handkerchief into one pocket, his snuffbox into another, and forgot his cane. He ran to the door in unaffected terror.

Where are all his fine airs before a real danger? Love, intrigue, diplomacy, were all driven from his mind; for he beheld that approaching which is the greatest peril and disaster known to social man. He saw a bore coming into the room!

In a wild thirst for novelty Pomander had once penetrated to Goodman's Fields Theatre; there he had unguardedly put a question to a carpenter behind the scene; a seedy-black poet instantly pushed the carpenter away, (down a trap it is thought,) and answered it in seven pages, and in continuation was so vaguely communicative that he drove Sir Charles back into the far west.

Sir Charles knew him again in a moment, and at sight of him bolted. They met at the door. "Ah, Mr. Triplet!" said the fugitive, "enchanted — to wish you good morning!" and he plunged into the hiding-places of the theatre.

"That is a very polite gentleman!" thought Triplet. He was followed by the call boy, to whom he was explaining that his avocations, though numerous, would not prevent his paying Mr. Rich the compliment of waiting all day in his greenroom, sooner than go without an answer to three important propositions, in which the town and the arts were concerned.

"What is your name?" said the boy of business to the man of words.

"Mr. Triplet," said Triplet.

"Triplet? There is something for you in the hall," said the urchin, and went off to fetch it.

"I knew it," said Triplet to himself; "they are accepted. There's a note in the hall to fix the reading." He then derided his own absurdity in having ever for a moment desponded. "Master of three arts, by each of which men grow fat, how was it possible he should starve all his days!"

He enjoyed a natural vanity for a few moments, and then came more generous feelings. What sparkling eyes there would be in Lambeth to-day! The butcher, at sight of Mr. Rich's handwriting, would give him credit. Jane should have a new gown.

But when his tragedies were played, and he paid!—El Dorado!—his children should be the neatest in the street. Lysimachus and Roxalana should learn the English language, cost what it might; sausages should be diurnal; and he himself would not be puffed up, fat, lazy. No; he would work all the harder, be affable as ever, and above all, never swamp the father, husband, and honest man, in the poet and the blackguard of sentiment.

Next his reflections took a business turn.

"These tragedies—the scenery? O, I shall have to paint it myself. The heroes? Well, they have nobody who will play them as I should. (This was true!) It will be hard work, all this; but then I shall be paid for it. I cannot go on this way; I must and will be paid separately for my branches."

Just as he came to this resolution, the boy returned with a brown-paper parcel, addressed to Mr. James Triplet. Triplet weighed it in his hand; it was heavy. "How is this?" cried he. "O, I see," said he; "these are the tragedies. He sends them to me for some trifling alterations; managers always do." Triplet then determined to adopt these alterations, if judicious; for, argued he, sensibly enough, "Managers are practical men; and we, in the heat of composition, sometimes (*sic?*) say more than is necessary, and become tedious."

With that he opened the parcel, and looked for Mr. Rich's communication; it was not in sight. He had to look between the leaves of the manuscripts for it; it was not there. He shook them: it did not fall out. He shook them as a dog shakes a rabbit; nothing!

The tragedies were returned without a word. It took him some time to realize the full weight of the blow; but at last he saw that the manager of the Theatre Royal, Covent Garden, declined to take a tragedy by Triplet into consideration, or bare examination.

He turned dizzy for a moment. Something

between a sigh and a cry escaped him, and he sank upon a covered bench that ran along the wall. His poor tragedies fell here and there upon the ground, and his head went down upon his hands, which rested on Mrs. Woffington's picture. His anguish was so sharp, it choked his breath; when he recovered it, his eye bent down upon the picture. "Ah, Jane," he groaned, "you know this villanous world better than I!" He placed the picture gently on the seat, (that picture must now be turned into bread,) and slowly stooped for his tragedies; they had fallen hither and thither; he had to crawl about for them; he was an emblem of all the humiliations letters endure.

As he went after them on all fours, more than one tear pattered on the dusty floor. Poor fellow! he was Triplet, and could not have died without tinging the death rattle with some absurdity; but after all, he was a father driven to despair; a castle builder, with his work rudely scattered; an artist, brutally crushed and insulted by a greater dunce than himself.

Faint, sick, and dark, he sat a moment on the

seat before he could find strength to go home and destroy all the hopes he had raised.

Whilst Triplet sat collapsed on the bench, fate sent into the room all in one moment, as if to insult his sorrow, a creature that seemed the goddess of gayety, impervious to a care. She swept in with a bold, free step, for she was rehearsing a man's part, and thundered without rant, but with a spirit and fire, and pace, beyond the conception of our poor tame actresses of 1852, these lines: —

> "'Now, by the joys
> Which my soul still has uncontrolled pursued,
> I would not turn aside from my least pleasure,
> Though all thy force were armed to bar my way;
> But, like the birds, great nature's happy commoners,
> Rifle the sweets ——'

"I beg — your par — don, sir!" holding the book on a level with her eye, she had nearly run over. "Two poets instead of one."

"Nay, madam," said Triplet, admiring, though sad, wretched, but polite, "pray continue. Happy the hearer, and still happier the author of verses so spoken. Ah!"

"Yes," replied the lady, "if you could persuade authors what we do for them, when we coax good music to grow on barren words. Are you an author, sir?" added she, slyly.

"In a small way, madam. I have here three trifles — tragedies."

Mrs. Woffington looked askant at them like a shy mare.

"Ah, madam!" said Triplet, in one of his insane fits, "if I might but submit them to such a judgment as yours?"

He laid his hand on them. It was as when a strange dog sees us go to take up a stone.

The actress recoiled.

"I am no judge of such things," cried she, hastily.

Triplet bit his lip. He could have killed her. It was provoking, people would rather be hung than read a manuscript. Yet what hopeless trash they will read in crowds, which was manuscript a day ago. *Les imbéciles!*

"No more is the manager of this theatre a judge of such things," cried the outraged quill driver, bitterly.

"What, has he accepted them?" said needle-tongue.

"No, madam, he has had them six months,

and see, madam, he has returned them me without a word."

Triplet's lip trembled.

"Patience, my good sir," was the merry reply. "Tragic authors should possess that, for they teach it to their audiences. Managers, sir, are like Eastern monarchs, inaccessible but to slaves and sultanas. Do you know I called upon Mr. Rich fifteen times before I could see him?"

"You, madam? Impossible!"

"O, it was years ago, and he has paid a hundred pounds for each of those little visits. Well, now, let me see, fifteen times; you must write twelve more tragedies, and then he will read *one*; and when he has read it, he will favor you with his judgment upon it; and when you have got that, you will have what all the world knows is not worth a farthing. He! he! he!

'And like the birds, gay Nature's happy commoners,
Rifle the sweets' — mum — mum — mum."

Her high spirits made Triplet sadder. To think that one word from this laughing lady would secure his work a hearing, and that he dared not ask her. She was up in the world, he was down. She was great, he was nobody. He felt a sort of chill at this woman — all brains and no heart. He took his picture and his plays under his arms and crept sorrowfully away.

The actress's eye fell on him as he went off like a fifth act. His Don Quixote face struck her. She had seen it before.

"Sir," said she.

"Madam," said Triplet, at the door.

"We have met before. There, don't speak, I'll tell you who you are. Yours is a face that has been good to me, and I never forget them."

"Me, madam!" said Triplet, taken aback. "I trust I know what is due to you better than to be good to you, madam," said he, in his confused way.

"To be sure!" cried she, "it is Mr. Triplet, good Mr. Triplet!" And this vivacious dame, putting her book down, seized both Triplet's hands and shook them.

He shook hers warmly in return out of excess of timidity, and dropped tragedies, and kicked at them convulsively when they were down, for fear they should be in her way, and his mouth opened, and his eyes glared.

"Mr. Triplet," said the lady, "do you remember an Irish orange girl you used to give sixpence to at Goodman's Fields, and pat her on the head and give her good advice, like a good old soul as you were? She took the sixpence."

"Madam," said Trip, recovering a grain of pomp, "singular as it may appear, I remember the young person; she was very engaging. I trust no harm hath befallen her, for methought I discovered, in spite of her brogue, a beautiful nature in her."

"Go along wid your blarney," answered a rich brogue; "an is it the comanther ye'd be putting on poor little Peggy?"

"O! O gracious!" gasped Triplet.

"Yes," was the reply; but into that "yes" she threw a whole sentence of meaning. "Fine cha-ney oran-ges!" chanted she, to put the matter beyond dispute.

"Am I really so honored as to have patted you on that queen-like head!" and he glared at it.

"On the same head which now I wear," replied she, pompously. "I kept it for the convaynience hintirely, only there's more in it. Well, Mr. Triplet, you see what Time has done for me; now, tell me whether he has been as kind to you: are you going to speak to me, Mr. Triplet?"

As a decayed hunter stands lean and disconsolate, head poked forward like a goose's, but if hounds sweep by his paddock in full cry, followed by horses who are what he was not, he does by reason of the good blood that is and will be in his heart, *dum spiritus hoss regit artus*, cock his ears, erect his tail, and trot fiery to his extremest hedge, and look over it, nostril distended, mane flowing, and neigh the hunt onward like a trumpet; so Triplet, who had manhood at bottom, instead of whining out his troubles in the ear of encouraging beauty, as a sneaking spirit would, perked up, and resolved to put the best face upon it all before so charming a creature of the other sex.

"Yes, madam," cried he, with the air of one who could have smacked his lips, "Providence has blessed me with an excellent wife and four charming children. My wife was Miss Chatterton: you remember her?"

"Yes! Where is she playing now?"

"Why, madam, her health is too weak for it."

"O! — You were scene painter. Do you still paint scenes?"

"With the pen, madam, not the brush: as the wags said, I transferred the distemper from my canvas to my imagination." And Triplet laughed uproariously.

When he had done, Mrs. Woffington, who had joined the laugh, inquired quietly whether his pieces had met with success.

"Eminent — in the closet; the stage is to come!" and he smiled absurdly again.

The lady smiled back.

"In short," said Triplet, recapitulating, "being blessed with health, and more tastes in the arts than most, and a cheerful spirit, I should be wrong, madam, to repine; and this day, in particular, is a happy one," added the rose colorist, "since the great Mrs. Woffington has deigned to remember me, and call me friend."

Such was Triplet's summary.

Mrs. Woffington drew out her memorandum book, and took down her summary of the crafty Triplet's facts. So easy is it for us Triplets to draw the wool over the eyes of women and Woffingtons.

"Triplet, discharged from scene painting; wife, no engagement; four children supported by his pen — that is to say, starving; lose no time!"

She closed her book, and smiled, and said, —

"I wish these things were comedies instead of trash-edies, as the French call them; we would cut one in half, and slice away the finest passages and then I would act in it; and you would see how the stage door would fly open at sight of the author."

"O Heaven!" said poor Trip, excited by this picture. "I'll go home, and write a comedy this moment."

"Stay!" said she; "you had better leave the tragedies with me."

"My dear madam! you will read them?"

"Ahem! I will make poor Rich read them."

"But, madam, he has rejected them."

"That is the first step. Reading them comes after, when it comes at all. What have you got in that green baize?"

"In this green baize?"

"Well, in this green baize, then."

"O, madam! nothing — nothing! To tell the truth, it is an adventurous attempt from memory.

I saw you play Silvia, madam; I was so charmed, that I came every night. I took your face home with me — forgive my presumption, madam — and I produced this faint adumbration, which I expose with diffidence."

So, then, he took the green baize off.

The color rushed into her face; she was evidently gratified. Poor, silly Mrs. Triplet was doomed to be right about this portrait.

"I will give you a sitting," said she. "You will find painting dull faces a better trade than writing dull tragedies. Work for other people's vanity, not your own; that is the art of art. And now I want Mr. Triplet's address."

"On the fly-leaf of each work, madam," replied that florid author, "and also at the foot of every page which contains a particularly brilliant passage, I have been careful to insert the address of James Triplet, painter, actor, and dramatist, and Mrs. Woffington's humble, devoted servant." He bowed ridiculously low, and moved towards the door; but something gushed across his heart, and he returned with long strides to her. "Madam!" cried he, with a janty manner, "you have inspired a son of Thespis with dreams of eloquence, you have tuned in a higher key a poet's lyre, you have tinged a painter's existence with brighter colors, and — and —— " His mouth worked still, but no more artificial words would come. He sobbed out, "And God in heaven bless you, Mrs. Woffington!" and ran out of the room.

Mrs. Woffington looked after him with interest, for this confirmed her suspicions; but suddenly her expression changed; she wore a look we have not yet seen upon her — it was a half-cunning, half-spiteful look: it was suppressed in a moment; she gave herself to her book, and presently Sir Charles Pomander sauntered into the room.

"Ah! what, Mrs. Woffington here?" said the diplomate.

"Sir Charles Pomander, I declare!" said the actress.

"I have just parted with an admirer of yours."

"I wish I could part with them all," was the reply.

"A pastoral youth, who means to win La Woffington by agricultural courtship — As shepherds woo in sylvan shades."

"'With oaten pipe the rustic maids,'"

quoth the Woffington, improvising.

The diplomate laughed, the actress laughed, and said, laughingly, "*Tell me what he says, word for word?*"

"It will only make you laugh."

"Well, and am I never to laugh, who provide so many laughs for you all?"

"*C'est juste.* You shall share the general merriment. Imagine a romantic soul, who adores you for *your simplicity!*"

"My simplicity! Am I so very simple?"

"No," said Sir Charles, monstrous dryly. "He says you are out of place on the stage, and wants to take the star from its firmament, and put it in a cottage."

"I am not a star," replied the Woffington, "I am only a meteor. And what does the man think I am to do without this, (here she imitated applause,) from my dear public's thousand hands?"

"You are to have this, (he mimicked a kiss,) from a single mouth, instead."

"He is mad! Tell me what more he says.

O, don't stop to invent; I should detect you; and you would only spoil this man."

He laughed conceitedly. "I should spoil him! Well then, he proposes to be your friend rather than your lover, and keep you from being talked of, he! he! instead of adding to your *éclat*."

"And if he is your friend, why don't you tell him my real character, and send him into the country?"

She said this rapidly and with an appearance of earnest. The diplomatist fell into the trap.

"I do," said he; "but he snaps his fingers at me, and common sense, and the world. I really think there is only one way to get rid of him, and with him of every annoyance."

"Ah! that would be nice."

"Delicious! I had the honor, madam, of laying certain proposals at your feet."

"O, yes — your letter, Sir Charles. I have only just had time to run my eye down it. Let us examine it together."

She took out the letter with a wonderful appearance of interest, and the diplomate allowed himself to fall into the absurd position to which she invited him. They put their two heads together over the letter.

"'A coach, a country house, pin money'— and I'm so tired of houses, and coaches, and pins. O, yes, here's something; what is this you offer me, up in this corner?"

Sir Charles inspected the place carefully, and announced that it was "his heart."

"And he can't even write it!" said she. "That word is 'earth.' Ah! well, you know best. There is your letter, Sir Charles."

She courtesied, returned him the letter, and resumed her study of Lothario.

"Favor me with your answer, madam," said her suitor.

"You have it," was the reply.

"Madam, I don't understand your answer,' said Sir Charles, stiffly.

"I can't find you answers and understandings too," was the lady-like reply. "You must beat my answer into your understanding whilst I beat this man's verse into mine.

"'And like the birds,' &c."

Pomander recovered himself a little; he laughed with quiet insolence. "Tell me," said he, "do you really refuse?"

"My good soul," said Mrs. Woffington, "why this surprise? Are you so ignorant of the stage and the world, as not to know that I refuse such offers as yours every week of my life."

"I know better," was the cool reply. She left it unnoticed.

"I have so many of these," continued she, "that I have begun to forget they are insults."

At this word the button broke off Sir Charles's foil.

"Insults, madam! they are the highest compliments you have left it in our power to pay you."

The other took the button off her foil.

"Indeed!" cried she, with well-feigned surprise. "O, I understand. To be your mistress, could be but a temporary disgrace; to be your wife, would be a lasting discredit," she continued. "And now, sir, having played your rival's game, and showed me your whole hand, (a light broke in upon our diplomate,) do something to recover the reputation of a man of the world. A gentleman is somewhere about in whom you have interested me by your lame satire; pray tell him I am in the greenroom, with no better companion than this bad poet."

Sir Charles clinched his teeth.

"I accept the delicate commission," replied he, "that you may see how easily the man of the world drops what the rustic is eager to pick up."

"That is better," said the actress, with a pro voking appearance of good humor. "You have a woman's tongue, if not her wit; but, my good soul," added she, with cool *hauteur*, "remember you have something to do of more importance than any thing you can say."

"I accept your courteous dismissal, madam," said Pomander, grinding his teeth. "I will send a carpenter for your swain; and I leave you."

He bowed to the ground.

"Thanks for the double favor, good Sir Charles."

She courtesied to the floor.

Feminine vengeance! He had come between her and her love. All very clever, Mrs. Actress; but was it wise?

"I am revenged," thought Mrs. Woffington, with a little feminine smirk.

"I will be revenged," vowed Pomander, clinching his teeth.

CHAPTER VII.

Compare a November day with a May day. They are not more unlike than a beautiful woman in company with a man she is indifferent to or averse, and the same woman with the man of her heart by her side.

At sight of Mr. Vane, all her coldness and *nonchalance* gave way to a gentle complacency; and when she spoke to him, her voice, so clear and cutting in the late *assaut d'armes*, sank of its own accord into the most tender, delicious tone imaginable.

Mr. Vane and she made love. He pleased her, and she desired to please him. My reader knows her wit, her *finesse*, her fluency; but he cannot conceive how godlike was her way of making love. I can put a few of the corpses of her words upon paper, but where are the heavenly tones — now calm and convincing, now soft and melancholy, now thrilling with tenderness, now glowing with the fiery eloquence of passion?

She told him that she knew the map of his face; that, for some days past, he had been subject to an influence adverse to her. She begged him, calmly, for his own sake, to distrust false friends, and judge her by his own heart, eyes, and judgment. He promised her he would.

"And I do trust you, in spite of them all," said he; "for your face is the shrine of sincerity and candor. I alone know you."

Then she prayed him to observe the heartlessness of his sex, and to say whether she had done ill to hide the riches of her heart from the cold and shallow, and to keep them all for one honest man, "who will be my friend, I hope," said she, "as well as my lover."

"Ah," said Vane, "that is my ambition."

"We actresses," said she, "make good the old proverb, 'Many lovers, but few friends.' And, O, 'tis we who need a friend. Will you be mine?"

Whilst he lived, he would.

In turn, he begged her to be generous, and tell him the way for him, Ernest Vane, inferior in wit and address to many of her admirers, to win her heart from them all.

This singular woman's answer is, I think, worth attention.

"Never act in my presence; never try to be eloquent or clever; never force a sentiment, or turn a phrase. Remember, I am the goddess of tricks. Do not descend to competition with me and the Pomanders of the world. At all littlenesses you will ever be awkward in my eyes And I am a woman. I must have a superior to love — lie open to my eye. Light itself is not more beautiful than the upright man, whose bosom is open to the day. O, yes! fear not you will be my superior, dear; for in me honesty has to struggle against the habits of my art and life. Be simple and sincere, and I shall love you, and bless the hour you shone upon my cold, artificial life. Ah, Ernest!" said she, fixing on his eyes her own, the fire of which melted into tenderness as she spoke, "be my friend. Come between me and the temptations of an unprotected life — the recklessness of a vacant heart."

He threw himself at her feet. He called her an angel. He told her he was unworthy of her, but that he would try and deserve her. Then he hesitated; and, trembling, he said, —

"I will be frank and loyal. Had I not better tell you every thing? You will not hate me for a confession I make myself."

"I shall like you better — O, so much better!"

"Then I will own to you ——"

"O, do not tell me you have ever loved before me! I could not bear to hear it!" cried this inconsistent personage.

The other weak creature needed no more.

"I see plainly I never loved but you," said he.

"Let me hear that only!" cried she; "I am jealous even of the past. Say you never loved but me: never mind whether it is true. My child, you do not even yet know love. Ernest, shall I make you love — as none of your sex ever loved — with heart, and brain, and breath, and life, and soul?"

With these rapturous words, she poured the soul of love into his eyes; he forgot every thing in the world but her; he dissolved in present happiness, and vowed himself hers forever; and she, for her part, bade him but retain her esteem, and no woman ever went farther in love than she would. She was a true epicure: she had learned that passion, vulgar in itself, is godlike when based upon esteem.

This tender scene was interrupted by the call boy, who brought Mrs. Woffington a note from the manager, informing her there would be no rehearsal. This left her at liberty, and she proceeded to take a somewhat abrupt leave of Mr. Vane. He was endeavoring to persuade her to let him be her companion until dinner time, (she was to be his guest,) when Pomander entered the room.

Mrs. Woffington, however, was not to be persuaded; she excused herself on the score of a duty which she said she had to perform, and whispering as she passed Pomander, "Keep your own counsel," she went out rather precipitately.

Vane looked slightly disappointed.

Sir Charles, who had returned to see whether (as he fully expected) she had told Vane every thing, — and who, at that moment, perhaps, would not have been sorry had Mrs. Woffington's lover called him to serious account, — finding it was not her intention to make mischief, and not choosing to publish his own defeat, dropped quietly into his old line, and determined to keep the lovers in sight, and play for revenge. He smiled, and said, "My good sir, nobody can hope to monopolize Mrs. Woffington : she has others to do justice to besides you."

To his surprise, Mr. Vane turned instantly round upon him, and looking him haughtily in the face, said, "Sir Charles Pomander, the settled malignity with which you pursue that lady is unmanly, and offensive to me, who love her Let our acquaintance cease here, if you please, or let her be sacred from your venomous tongue."

Sir Charles bowed stiffly, and replied, that it was only due to himself to withdraw a protection so little appreciated.

The two friends were in the very act of separating forever, when who should run in but Pompey, the renegade. He darted up to Sir Charles, and said, "Massa Pomannah, she in a coach, going to 10, Hercules Buildings. I'm in a hurry, Massa Pomannah."

"Where?" cried Pomander. "Say that again."

"10, Hercules Buildings, Lambeth. Me in a hurry, Massa Pomannah."

"Faithful child, there's a guinea for thee. Fly!"

The slave flew, and taking a short cut, caught

and fastened on to the slow vehicle in the Strand.

"It is a house of rendez-vous," said Sir Charles, half to himself, half to Mr. Vane. He repeated, in triumph, "It is a house of rendez-vous." He then, recovering his *sang froid*, and treating it all as a matter of course, explained that at 10, Hercules Buildings, was a fashionable shop, with entrances from two streets; that the best Indian scarfs and shawls were sold there, and that ladies kept their carriages waiting an immense time in the principal street, whilst they were supposed to be in the shop, or the show room. He then went on to say, that he had only this morning heard, that the intimacy between Mrs. Woffington and a Colonel Murthwaite, although publicly broken off for prudential reasons, was still clandestinely carried on. She had, doubtless, slipped away to meet the colonel.

Mr. Vane turned pale.

"No! I will not suspect. I will not dog her like a bloodhound," cried he.

"I will!" said Pomander.

"You! By what right?"

"The right of curiosity. I will know whether it is you who are imposed on; or whether you are right, and all the world is deceived in this woman."

He ran out; but for all his speed, when he got into the street, there was the jealous lover at his elbow. They darted with all speed into the Strand; got a coach. Sir Charles, on the box, gave Jehu a guinea, and took the reins — and by a Niagara of whip-cord they attained Lambeth; and, at length, to his delight, Pomander saw another coach before him with a gold-laced black slave behind it. The coach stopped; and the slave came to the door. The shop in question was a few hundred yards distant. The adroit Sir Charles not only stopped, but turned his coach, and let the horses crawl back towards London; he also flogged the side panels to draw the attention of Mr. Vane. That gentleman looked through the little circular window at the back of the vehicle, and saw a lady paying the coachman. There was no mistaking her figure. This lady, then, followed at a distance by her slave, walked on towards Hercules Buildings; and it was his miserable fate to see her look uneasily round, and at last glide in at a side door, close to the silk mercer's shop.

The carriage stopped. Sir Charles came himself to the door.

"Now, Vane," said he, "before I consent to go any farther in this business, you must promise me to be cool and reasonable. I abhor absurdity; and there must be no swords drawn for this little hypocrite."

"I submit to no dictation," said Vane, white as a sheet.

"You have benefited so far by my knowl edge," said the other, politely; "let me, who am self-possessed, claim some influence with you?"

"Forgive me!" said poor Vane. "My ang — my sorrow that such an angel should be a monster of deceit." He could say no more.

They walked to the shop.

"How she peeped this way and that," said Pomander, "sly little Woffy!"

"No! on second thoughts," said he, "it is the other street we must reconnoitre; and if we don't see her there, we will enter the shop, and by dint of this purse, we shall soon untie the knot of the Woffington riddle."

Vane leaned heavily on his tormentor.

"I am faint," said he.

"Lean on me, my dear friend," said Sir Charles. "Your weakness will leave you in the next street."

In the next street they discovered — nothing. In the shop they found — no Mrs. Woffington. They returned to the principal street. Vane began to hope there was no positive evidence. Suddenly three stories up a fiddle was heard. Pomander took no notice, but Vane turned red; this put Sir Charles upon the scent.

"Stay!" said he. "Is not that an Irish tune?"

Vane groaned. He covered his face with his hands, and hissed out, —

"It is her favorite tune."

"Aha!" said Pomander. "Follow me."

They crept up the stairs, Pomander in advance; they heard the signs of an Irish orgie — a rattling jig played, and danced with the inspiriting interjections of that frolicsome nation. These sounds ceased after a while, and Pomander laid his hand on his friend's shoulder.

"I prepare you," said he, "for what you are sure to see. This woman was an Irish bricklayer's daughter, and 'what is bred in the bone

12

never comes out of the flesh.' You will find her sitting on some Irishman's knee, whose limbs are ever so much stouter than yours. You are the man of her head, and this is the man of her heart. These things would be monstrous if they were not common; incredible, if we did not see them every day. But this poor fellow, whom probably she deceives as well as you, is not to be sacrificed like a dog to your unjust wrath: he is as superior to her as you are to him."

"I will commit no violence," said Vane. "I still hope she is innocent."

Pomander smiled, and said he hoped so too.

"And if she is what you think, I will but show her she is known; and blaming myself as much as her, — O, yes, more than her — I will go down this night to Shropshire, and never speak word to her again in this world or the next."

"Good!" said Sir Charles.

"'Le bruit est pour le fat, la plainte est pour le sot,
L'honnête homme trompé s'éloigne et ne dit mot.'

Are you ready?"

"Yes."

"Then follow me."

Turning the handle gently, he opened the door like lightning, and was in the room. Vane's head peered over his shoulder. She was actually there!

For once in her life the cautious, artful woman was taken by surprise. She gave a little scream, and turned as red as fire. But Sir Charles surprised somebody else even more than he did poor Mrs. Woffington.

It would be impertinent to tantalize my reader; but I flatter myself this history is not written with power enough to do that; and I may venture to leave him to guess whom Sir Charles Pomander surprised more than he did the actress, while I go back for the lagging sheep.

CHAPTER VIII.

James Triplet, water in his eye, but fire in his heart, went home on wings. Arrived there, he anticipated curiosity by informing all hands he should answer no questions. Only in the intervals of a work, which was to take the family out of all its troubles, he should gradually unfold a tale, verging on the marvellous — a tale whose only fault was, that fiction, by which alone the family could hope to be great, paled beside it. He then seized some sheets of paper, fished out some old dramatic sketches, and a list of *dramatis personæ,* prepared years ago, and plunged into a comedy. As he wrote, true to his promise, he painted, Triplet-wise, that story which we have coldly related, and made it appear to all but Mrs. Triplet, that he was under the *tutela,* or express protection, of Mrs. Woffington, who would push his fortunes until the only difficulty would be to keep arrogance out of the family heart.

Mrs. Triplet groaned aloud. "You have brought the picture home, I see," said she.

"Of course I have. She is going to give me a sitting."

"At what hour of what day?" said Mrs Triplet, with a world of meaning.

"She did not say," replied Triplet, avoiding his wife's eye.

"I know she did not," was the answer. "I would rather you had brought me the ten shillings than this fine story," said she.

"Wife!" said Triplet, "don't put me into a a frame of mind in which successful comedies are not written." He scribbled away; but his wife's despondency told upon the man of disappointments. Then he stuck fast; then he became fidgety.

"Do keep those children quiet," said the father.

"Hush, my dears," said the mother; "let your father write. Comedy seems to give you more trouble than tragedy, James," added she, soothingly.

"Yes," was his answer. "Sorrow comes, somehow, more natural to me; but for all that I have got a bright thought, Mrs. Triplet. Listen, all of you. You see, Jane, they are all at a sumptuous banquet, all the *dramatis personæ,* except the poet."

Triplet went on writing, and reading his work out: "Music, sparkling wine, massive plate, rose water in the hand glasses, soup, fish — shall I have three sorts of fish? I will; they are cheap in this market. Ah, Fortune, you wretch, here at least I am your master, and I'll make you know it — venison," wrote Triplet, with a malicious grin, "game, pickles, and provocatives in the centre of the table, then up jumps one of the guests, and says he ——"

"O dear, I am so hungry!"

This was not from the comedy, but from one of the boys.

"And so am I," cried a girl.

"That is an absurd remark, Lysimachus," said Triplet, with a suspicious calmness.

"How can a boy be hungry three hours after breakfast?"

"But, father, there was no breakfast for breakfast."

"Now I ask you, Mrs. Triplet," appealed the

author, "how am I to write comic scenes if you let Lysimachus and Roxalana here put the heavy business in every five minutes?"

"Forgive them; the poor things are hungry."

"Then let them be hungry in another room," said the irritated scribe. "They shan't cling round my pen, and paralyze it just when it is going to make all our fortunes; but you women," snapped Triplet the Just, "have no consideration for people's feelings. Send them all to bed, every man jack of them!"

Finding the conversation taking this turn, the brats raised a unanimous howl.

Triplet darted a fierce glance at them. "Hungry, hungry!" cried he; "is that a proper expression to use before a father who is sitting down here all gayety (scratching wildly with his pen) and hilarity (scratch) to write a com — com —" he choked a moment, then in a very different voice, all sadness and tenderness, he said, "Where's the youngest? where's Lucy? As if I didn't know you are hungry."

Lucy came to him directly. He took her on his knee, pressed her gently to his side, and wrote silently. The others were still.

"Father," said Lucy, aged five, the germ of a woman, "I am not tho very hungry."

"And I am not hungry at all," said bluff Lysimachus, taking his sister's cue; then going upon his own tact he added, "I had a great piece of bread and butter yesterday!"

"Wife, they will drive me mad!" and he dashed at the paper.

The second boy explained to his mother *sotto voce,* "Mother, he *made* us hungry out of his book."

"It is a beautiful book," said Lucy; "is it a cookery book?"

Triplet roared. "Do you hear that?" inquired he, all trace of ill humor gone. "Wife," he resumed, after a gallant scribble, "I took that sermon I wrote."

"And beautiful it was, James. I'm sure it quite cheered me up with thinking that we shall all be dead before so very long."

"Well, the reverend gentleman would not have it. He said it was too hard upon sin. 'You run at the devil like a mad bull,' said he. 'Sell it in Lambeth, sir; *here* calmness and decency are before every thing,' says he. 'My congregation expect to go to heaven down hill. Perhaps the chaplain of Newgate might give you a crown for it,' said he; " and Triplet dashed viciously at the paper. "Ah!" sighed he, "if my friend Mrs. Woffington would but drop these stupid comedies and take to tragedy, this house would soon be all smiles."

"O James!" replied Mrs. Triplet, almost peevishly, "how can you expect any thing but fine words from that woman? You won't believe what all the world says. You will trust to your own good heart."

"I haven't a good heart," said the poor, honest fellow. "I spoke like a brute to you just now."

"Never mind, James," said the woman; "I wonder how you put up with me at all, a sick, useless creature. I often wish to die, for your sake. I know you would do better. I am such a weight round your neck."

The man made no answer, but he put Lucy gently down, and went to the woman, and took her forehead to his bosom, and held it there; and after a while returned with silent energy to his comedy.

"Play us a tune on the fiddle, father."

"Ay, do, husband. That helps you often in your writing."

Lysimachus brought him the fiddle, and Triplet essayed a merry tune; but it came out so doleful, that he shook his head, and laid the instrument down. Music must be in the heart, or it will come out of the fingers — notes, not music.

"No," said he; "let us be serious, and finish this comedy slap off. Perhaps it hitches because I forgot to invoke the comic muse. She must be a black-hearted jade, if she doesn't come with merry notions to a poor devil, starving in the midst of his hungry little ones."

"We are past help from heathen goddesses," said the woman. "We must pray to Heaven to look down upon us and our children."

The man looked up with a very bad expression on his countenance.

"You forget," said he, sullenly, "our street is very narrow, and the opposite houses are very high."

"James!"

"How can Heaven be expected to see what

honest folk endure in so dark a hole as this?" cried the man, fiercely.

"James," said the woman, with fear and sorrow, "what words are these?"

The man rose, and flung his pen upon the floor.

"Have we given honesty a fair trial — yes or no?"

"No!" said the woman, without a moment's hesitation; "not till we die, as we have lived. Heaven is higher than the sky. Children," said she, lest, perchance, her husband's words should have harmed their young souls, "the sky is above the earth, and Heaven is higher than the sky; and Heaven is just."

"I suppose it is so," said the man, a little cowed by her. "Every body says so. I think so, at bottom, myself; but I can't see it. I want to see it, but I can't!" cried he, fiercely. "Have my children offended Heaven? They will starve — they will die. If I was Heaven, I'd be just, and send an angel to take these children's part. They cried to me for bread; I had no bread, so I gave them hard words. The moment I had done that, I knew it was all over. God knows it took a long while to break my heart; but it is broken at last; quite, quite broken, broken, broken!"

And the poor thing laid his head upon the table, and sobbed beyond all power of restraint. The children cried round him, scarce knowing why; and Mrs. Triplet could only say, "My poor husband!" and prayed and wept upon the couch where she lay.

It was at this juncture that a lady, who had knocked gently and unheard, opened the door, and with a light step entered the apartment; but no sooner had she caught sight of Triplet's anguish, than saying hastily, "Stay, I forgot something," she made as hasty an exit.

This gave Triplet a moment to recover himself; and Mrs. Woffington, whose lynx eye had comprehended all at a glance, and who had determined at once what line to take, came flying in again, saying,—

"Wasn't somebody inquiring for an angel? Here I am. See, Mr. Triplet!" and she showed him a note, which said, "Madam, you are an angel. From a perfect stranger," explained she; "so it must be true."

"Mrs. Woffington," said Mr. Triplet to his wife.

Mrs. Woffington planted herself in the middle of the floor, and with a comical glance, setting her arms akimbo, uttered a shrill whistle.

"Now you will see another angel — there are two sorts of them."

Pompey came in with a basket. She took it from him.

"Lucifer, avaunt!" cried she, in a terrible tone, that drove him to the wall; "and wait outside the door," added she, conversationally.

"I heard you were ill, ma'am, and I have brought you some physic — black draughts from Burgundy;" and she smiled. And recovered from their first surprise, young and old began to thaw beneath that witching, irresistible smile. "Mrs. Triplet, I have come to give your husband a sitting; will you allow me to eat my little luncheon with you? I am so hungry!" Then she clapped her hands, and in ran Pompey. She sent him for a pie she professed to have fallen in love with at the corner of the street.

"Mother," said Alcibiades, "will the lady give me a bit of her pie?"

"Hush! you rude boy!" cried the mother.

"She is not much of a lady if she does not," cried Mrs. Woffington. "Now, children, first let us look at—ahem—a comedy. Nineteen *dramatis personæ!* What do you say, children, shall we cut out seven, or nine? that is the question. You can't bring your armies into our drawing rooms, Mr. Dagger-and-bowl. Are you the Marlborough of comedy? Can you marshal battalions on a Turkey carpet, and make gentlefolks witty in platoons? What is this in the first act? A duel, and both wounded! You butcher!"

"They are not to die, ma'am!" cried Triplet, deprecatingly; "upon my honor," said he, solemnly, spreading his hands on his bosom.

"Do you think I'll trust their lives with you? No! Give me a pen: this is the way *we* run people through the body." Then she wrote ("business." Araminta looks out of the garret window. Combatants drop their swords, put their hands to their hearts, and stagger off O. P. and P. S.) "Now, children, who helps me to lay the cloth?"

"I!"

"And I!" (The children run to the cupboard.)

Mrs. Triplet, (half rising.) — "Madam, I — can't think of allowing you."

Mrs. Woffington replied, "Sit down, madam, or I must use brute force. If you are ill, be ill — till I make you well. Twelve plates, quick! Twenty-four knives, quicker! Forty-eight forks, quickest!" She met the children with the cloth and laid it; then she met them again and laid knives and forks, all at full gallop, which mightily excited the bairns. Pompey came in with the pie; Mrs. Woffington took it and set it before Triplet.

Mrs. Woffington. — "Your coat, Mr. Triplet, if you please."

Mr. Triplet. — "My coat, madam!"

Mrs. Woffington. — "Yes, off with it — there's a hole in it — and carve. Then she whipped to the other end of the table and stitched like wildfire. "Be pleased to cast your eyes on that, Mrs. Triplet. Pass it to the lady, young gentleman. Fire away, Mr. Triplet; never mind us women. Woffington's housewife, ma'am, fearful to the eye, only it holds every thing in the world, and there is a small space for every thing else — to be returned by the bearer. Thank you, sir." (Stitches away like lightning at the coat.) "Eat away, children! now is your time: when once I begin, the pie will soon end; I do every thing so quick."

Roxalana. — "The lady sews quicker than you, mother."

Woffington. — "Bless the child, don't come so near my sword arm; the needle will go into your eye, and out at the back of your head."

This nonsense made the children giggle.

"The needle will be lost — the child no more — enter undertaker — house turned topsy-turvy — father shows Woffington to the door — off she goes with a face as long and dismal as some people's comedies — no names — crying fine cha-ney oran-ges."

The children, all but Lucy, screeched with laughter.

Lucy said, gravely, —

"Mother, the lady is very funny!"

"You will be as funny, when you are as well paid for it."

This just hit poor Trip's notion of humor;

and he began to choke, with his mouth full of pie.

"James, take care," said Mrs. Triplet, sad and solemn.

James looked up.

"My wife is a good woman, madam," said he, "but deficient in an important particular."

"O James!"

"Yes, my dear. I regret to say you have no sense of humor; nummore than a cat, Jane."

"What! because the poor thing can't laugh at your comedy?"

"No, ma'am; but she laughs at nothing."

"Try her with one of your tragedies, my lad?"

"I am sure, James," said the poor, good, lackadaisical woman, "if I don't laugh, it is not for want of the will. I used to be a very hearty laugher," whined she; "but I haven't laughed this two years."

"O, indeed!" said the Woffington. "Then the next two years you shall do nothing else."

"Ah, madam!" said Triplet, "that passes the art even of the great comedian."

"Does it?" said the actress, coolly.

LUCY. — "She is not a comedy lady. You don't ever cry, pretty lady?"

WOFFINGTON, (ironically.) — "O, of course not."

LUCY, (confidentially.) — "Comedy is crying. Father cried all the time he was writing his one."

Triplet turned red as fire.

"Hold your tongue," said he; "I was bursting with merriment. Wife, our children talk too much; they put their noses into every thing, and criticize their own father."

"Unnatural offspring!" laughed the visitor.

"And when they take up a notion, Socrates couldn't convince them to the contrary. For instance, madam, all this morning they thought fit to assume that they were starving."

"So we were," said Lysimachus, "until the angel came, and the devil went for the pie."

"There — there — there! Now, you mark my words; we shall never get that idea out of their heads ——"

"Until," said Mrs. Woffington, lumping a huge cut of pie into Roxalana's plate, "we put a very different idea into their stomachs." This and the look she cast on Mrs. Triplet, fairly caught that good, though sombre personage. She giggled, put her hand to her face, and said, "I'm sure I ask your pardon, ma'am."

It was no use; the comedian had determined they should all laugh, and they were made to laugh. Then she rose, and showed them how to drink healths *à la Française;* and keen were her little admirers, to touch her glass with theirs. And the pure wine she had brought did Mrs. Triplet much good, too; though not so much as the music and sunshine of her face and voice. Then, when their stomachs were full of good food, and the soul of the grape tingled in their veins, and their souls glowed under her great magnetic power, she suddenly seized the fiddle, and showed them another of her enchantments. She put it on her knee, and played a tune that would have made gout, colic, and phthisic dance upon their last legs. She played to the eye as well as to the ear, with such a smart gesture of the bow, and such a radiance of face as she looked at them, that whether the music came out of her wooden shell, or her horsehair wand, or her bright self, seemed doubtful. They pranced on their chairs; they could not keep still. She jumped up; so did they. She gave a wild Irish horroo. She put the fiddle in Triplet's hand.

"The wind that shakes the barley, ye divil!" cried she.

Triplet went *hors de lui*; he played like Paganini, or an intoxicated demon. Woffington covered the buckle in gallant style; she danced, the children danced. Triplet fiddled and danced, and flung his limbs in wild dislocation; the wine glasses danced; and last, Mrs. Triplet was observed to be bobbing about on her sofa, in a monstrous absurd way, droning out the tune, and playing her hands with mild enjoyment, all to herself. Woffington pointed out this pantomimic soliloquy to the two boys, with a glance full of fiery meaning. This was enough: with a fiendish yell, they fell upon her, and tore her, shrieking, off the sofa. And lo! when she was once launched, she danced up to her husband, and set to him with a meek deliberation, that was as funny as any part of the scene. So then the mover of all this slipped on one side, and let the stone of merriment roll — and roll it did; there was no swimming, sprawling, or irrelevant frisking; their feet struck the ground for every note of the fiddle, pat as its echo, their faces shone, their hearts leaped, and their poor frozen natures came out, and warmed themselves at the glowing melody; a great sunbeam had come into their abode, and these human motes danced in it. The elder ones recovered their gravity first; they sat down breathless, and put their hands to their hearts; they looked at one another, and then at the goddess who had revived them. Their first feeling was wonder; were they the same, who, ten minutes ago, were weeping together? Yes! ten minutes ago they were rayless, joyless, hopeless. Now the sun was in their hearts, and sorrow and sighing were fled, as fogs disperse before the god of day. It was magical; could a mortal play upon the soul of man, woman, and child like this? Happy Woffington! and suppose this was more than half acting, but such acting as Triplet never dreamed of; and to tell the honest, simple truth, I myself should not have suspected it; but children are sharper than one would think, and Alcibiades Triplet told, in after years, that when they were all dancing except the lady, he caught sight of her face — and it was quite, quite grave, and even sad; but as often as she saw him look at her, she smiled at him so gayly he couldn't believe it was the same face.

If it was art, glory be to such art so worthily applied! and honor to such creatures as this, that come like sunshine into poor men's houses, and tune drooping hearts to daylight and hope!

The wonder of these worthy people soon changed to gratitude. Mrs. Woffington stopped their mouths at once.

"No, no!" cried she; "if you really love me, no scenes; I hate them. Tell these brats to kiss me, and let me go. I must sit for my picture after dinner; it is a long way to Bloomsbury Square."

The children needed no bidding; they clustered round her, and poured out their innocent hearts as children only do.

"I shall pray for you after father and mother," said one.

"I shall pray for you after daily bread," said Lucy, "because we were *tho* hungry till you came!"

"My poor children!" cried Woffington; and hard to grown-up actors, as she called us, but sensitive to children, she fairly melted as she embraced them. It was at this precise juncture that the door was unceremoniously opened, and the two gentlemen burst upon the scene!

My reader now guesses whom Sir Charles Pomander surprised more than he did Mrs. Woffington. He could not for the life of him comprehend what she was doing, and what was her ulterior object. The *nil admirari* of the fine gentleman deserted him, and he gazed openmouthed, like the veriest chaw-bacon.

The actress, unable to extricate herself in a moment from the children, stood there like Charity, in New College Chapel, whilst the mother kissed her hand, and the father quietly dropped tears, like some leaden water-god in the middle of a fountain.

Vane turned hot and cold by turns, with joy and shame. Pomander's genius came to the aid of their embarrassment.

"Follow my lead," whispered he. "What! Mrs. Woffington here!" cried he; then he advanced business-like to Triplet. "We are aware, sir, of your various talents, and are come to make a demand on them. I, sir, am the unfortunate possessor of frescoes; time has impaired their indelicacy; no man can restore it as you can."

"Augh! Sir! sir!" said the gratified goose.

"My Cupid's bows are walking-sticks, and my Venus's noses are snubbed. You must set all that straight, on your own terms, Mr. Triplet."

"In a single morning all shall bloom again, sir! Whom would you wish them to resemble in feature? I have lately been praised for my skill in portraiture." (Glancing at Mrs. Woffington.)

"O," said Pomander, carelessly, "you need not go far for Venuses and Cupids, I suppose?"

"I see, sir: my wife and children. Thank you, sir; thank you."

Pomander stared; Mrs. Woffington laughed.

Now it was Vane's turn.

"Let me have a copy of verses from your pen. I shall have five pounds at your disposal for them."

"The world has found me out," thought Triplet, blinded by his vanity. "The subject, sir?"

"No matter," said Vane; "no matter."

"O, of course, it does not matter to me," said Triplet, with some *hauteur*, and assuming poetic omnipotence. "Only, when one knows the subject, one can sometimes make the verses apply better."

"Write then, since you are so confident, upon Mrs. Woffington."

"Ah! that is a subject! They shall be ready in an hour!" cried Trip, in whose imagination Parnassus was a raised counter. He had in a teacup some lines on Venus and Mars, which he could not but feel would fit Thalia and Crœsus, or Genius and Envy, equally well. "In one hour, sir," said Triplet, "the article shall be executed, and delivered at your house."

Mrs. Woffington called Vane to her, with an engaging smile. A month ago, he would have hoped she would not have penetrated him and Sir Charles; but he knew her better now. He came trembling.

"Look me in the face, Mr. Vane," said she gently, but firmly.

"I cannot!" said he. "How can I ever look you in the face again?"

"Ah, you disarm me! But I must strike you, or this will never end. Did I not promise that when you had earned my esteem, I would tell you — what no mortal knows — Ernest, my whole story? I delay the confession: it will cost me so many blushes — so many tears! And yet I hope, if you knew all, you would pity and forgive me. Meantime, did I ever tell you a falsehood?"

"O, no!"

"Why doubt me then, when I tell you that I hold all your sex cheap, but you? Why suspect me of Heaven knows what, at the dictation of a heartless, brainless fop — on the word of a known liar, like the world?"

Black lightning flashed from her glorious eyes, as she administered this royal rebuke. Vane felt what a poor creature he was, and his face showed such burning shame and contrition, that he obtained his pardon without speaking.

"There," said she, kindly, "do not let us torment one another. I forgive you. Let me make you happy, Ernest. Is that a great favor to ask? I can make you happier than your brightest dream of happiness, if you will let yourself be happy."

They rejoined the others; but Vane turned his back on Pomander, and would not look at him.

"Sir Charles," said Mrs. Woffington, gayly; for she scorned to admit the fine gentleman to the rank of a permanent enemy, "you will be of our party, I trust, at dinner?"

"Why, no, madam; I fear I cannot give myself that pleasure to-day." Sir Charles did not choose to swell the triumph. "Mr. Vane, good day!" said he, rather dryly. "Mr. Triplet — madam — your most obedient!" and, self-possessed at top, but at bottom crestfallen, he bowed himself away.

Sir Charles, however, on descending the stair and gaining the street, caught sight of a horseman, riding uncertainly about, and making his horse curvet to attract attention.

He soon recognized one of his own horses, and upon it the servant he had left behind to dog that poor innocent country lady. The servant sprang off his horse and touched his hat. He informed his master that he had kept with the carriage until ten o'clock this morning, when he had ridden away from it at Barnet, having duly pumped the servants as opportunity offered.

"Who is she?" cried Sir Charles.

"Wife of a Cheshire squire, Sir Charles," was the reply.

"His name? Whither goes she in town?'

"Her name is Mrs. Vane, Sir Charles. She is going to her husband."

"Curious!" cried Sir Charles. "I wish she had no husband. No! I wish she came from Shropshire;" and he chuckled at the notion.

"If you please, Sir Charles," said the man, "is not Willoughby in Cheshire?"

"No," cried his master; "it is in Shropshire. What! eh! Five guineas for you if that lady comes from Willoughby in Shropshire."

"That is where she comes from then, Sir Charles, and she is going to Bloomsbury Square."

"How long have they been married?"

"Not more than twelve months, Sir Charles."

Pomander gave the man ten guineas instead of five on the spot.

Reader, it was too true! Mr. Vane — the good, the decent, the church-goer — Mr. Vane, whom Mrs. Woffington had selected to improve her morals — Mr. Vane was a married man!

CHAPTER IX.

As soon as Pomander had drawn his breath and realized this discovery, he darted up stairs, and with all the demure calmness he could assume, told Mr. Vane, whom he met descending, that he was happy to find his engagements permitted him to join the party in Bloomsbury Square. He then flung himself upon his servant's horse.

Like Iago, he saw the indistinct outline of a glorious and a most malicious plot; it lay crude in his head and heart at present; thus much he saw clearly, that if he could time Mrs. Vane's arrival so that she should pounce upon the Woffington at her husband's table, he might be present at and enjoy the public discomfiture of a man and woman who had wounded his vanity. Bidding his servant make the best of his way to Bloomsbury Square, Sir Charles galloped in that direction himself, intending first to inquire whether Mrs. Vane was arrived, and if not, to ride towards Islington and meet her. His plan was frustrated by an accident; galloping round a corner, his horse did not change his leg cleverly, and the pavement being also loose, slipped and fell on his side, throwing his rider upon the *trottoir*. The horse got up and trembled violently, but was unhurt. The rider lay motionless, except that his legs quivered on the pavement. They took him up and conveyed him into a druggist's shop, the master of which practised chirurgery. He had to be sent for; and before he could be found, Sir Charles recovered his reason — so much so that when the chirurgeon approached with his fleam to bleed him, according to the practice of the day, the patient drew his sword, and assured the other he would let out every drop of blood in his body if he touched him.

He of the shorter but more lethal weapon hastily retreated. Sir Charles flung a guinea on the counter, and mounting his horse, rode him off rather faster than before this accident.

There was a dead silence!

"I believe that gentleman to be the devil!"

said a thoughtful bystander. The crowd (it was a century ago) assented, *nem. con.*

Sir Charles, arrived in Bloomsbury Square, found that the whole party was assembled. He therefore ordered his servant to parade before the door, and if he saw Mrs. Vane's carriage enter the square, to let him know, if possible, before she should reach the house. On entering he learned that Mr. Vane and his guests were in the garden, (a very fine one,) and joined them there.

Mrs. Vane demands another chapter, in which I will tell the reader who she was, and what excuse her husband had for his *liaison* with Margaret Woffington.

CHAPTER X.

Mabel Chester was the beauty and toast of South Shropshire. She had refused the hand of half the country squires in a circle of some dozen miles, till at last Mr. Vane became her suitor. Besides a handsome face and person, Mr. Vane had accomplishments his rivals did not possess. He read poetry to her on mossy banks, an hour before sunset, and awakened sensibilities, which her other suitors shocked, and they them.

The lovely Mabel had a taste for beautiful things, without any excess of that severe quality called judgment.

I will explain. If you or I, reader, had read to her in the afternoon amidst the smell of roses and eglantine, the chirp of the mavis, the hum of bees, the twinkling of butterflies, and the tinkle of distant sheep, something that combined all these sights, and sounds, and smells — say Milton's musical picture of Eden, P. L., lib. 3, and after that "Triplet on Kew," she would have instantly pronounced in favor of "Eden;" but if *we* had read her "Milton," and Mr. Vane had read her "Triplet," she would have as unhesitatingly preferred "Kew" to "Paradise."

She was a true daughter of Eve; the lady who, when an angel was telling her and her husband the truths of heaven in heaven's own music, slipped away into the kitchen, because she preferred hearing the story at second hand, encumbered with digressions, and in mortal but marital accents.

When her mother, who guarded Mabel like a dragon, told her Mr. Vane was not rich enough, and she really must not give him so many opportunities, Mabel cried and embraced the dragon, and said, "O mother!" The dragon, finding her ferocity dissolving, tried to shake her off, but the goose would cry and embrace the dragon till it melted.

By and by Mr. Vane's uncle died suddenly, and left him the great Stoken Church estate, and a trunk full of Jacobuses and Queen Anne's guineas — his own hoard and his father's — then the dragon spake comfortably, and said, —

"My child, he is now the richest man in

Shropshire. He will not think of you now; so steel your heart."

Then Mabel, contrary to all expectations, did not cry; but with flushing cheek, pledged her life upon Ernest's love and honor. And Ernest, as soon as the funeral, &c., left him free, galloped to Mabel, to talk of our good fortune. The dragon had done him injustice: that was not his weak point. So they were married! and they were very, very happy. But one month after, the dragon died, and that was their first grief; but they bore it together.

And Vane was not like the other Shropshire squires. His idea of pleasure was something his wife could share. He still rode, walked, and sat with her, and read to her, and composed songs for her, and about her, which she played and sang prettily enough, in her quiet, lady-like way, and in a voice of honey dropping from the comb. Then she kept a keen eye upon him; and when she discovered what dishes he liked, she superintended those herself; and observing that he never failed to eat of a certain lemon pudding the dragon had originated, she always made this pudding herself, and she never told her husband she made it.

The first seven months of their marriage were more like blue sky than brown earth; and if any one had told Mabel that her husband was a mortal, and not an angel sent to her, that her days and nights might be unmixed, uninterrupted heaven, she could hardly have realized the information.

When a vexatious litigant began to contest the will by which Mr. Vane was Lord of Stoken Church, and Mr. Vane went up to London to concert the proper means of defeating this attack, Mrs. Vane would gladly have compounded by giving the man two or three thousand acres, or the whole estate, if he wouldn't take less, not to rob her of her husband for a month; but she was docile as she was amorous; so she cried (out of sight) a week, and let her darling go, with every misgiving a loving heart could have; but one! and that one, her own heart told her, was impossible.

The month rolled away; no symptom of a return. For this Mr. Vane was not, in fact, to blame; but, towards the end of the next month, business became a convenient excuse. When three months had passed, Mrs. Vane became unhappy. She thought he too must feel the separation. She offered to come to him. He answered uncandidly. He urged the length, the fatigue of the journey. She was silenced; but some time later, she began to take a new view of his objections. "He is so self-denying," said she. "Dear Ernest, he longs for me; but he thinks it selfish to let me travel so far alone to see him."

Full of this idea, she yielded to her love. She made her preparations, and wrote to him that if he did not forbid her peremptorily, he must expect to see her at his breakfast table in a very few days.

Mr. Vane concluded this was a jest, and did not answer this letter at all.

Mrs. Vane started. She travelled with all speed; but coming to a halt at ——, she wrote to her husband that she counted on being with him at four of the clock on Thursday.

This letter preceded her arrival by a few hours. It was put into his hand at the same time with a note from Mrs. Woffington, telling him she should be at a rehearsal at Covent Garden. Thinking his wife's letter would keep, he threw it on one side into a sort of a tray; and after a hurried breakfast, went out of his house to the theatre. He returned, as we are aware, with Mrs. Woffington; and also, at her request, with Mr. Cibber, for whom they called on their way. He had forgotten his wife's letter, and was entirely occupied with his guests.

Sir Charles Pomander joined them, and found Mr. Colander, the head domestic of the London establishment, cutting with a pair of scissors every flower Mrs. Woffington fancied — that lady having a passion for flowers.

Colander, during his temporary absence from the interior, had appointed James Burdock to keep the house, and receive the two remaining guests, should they arrive.

This James Burdock was a faithful old country servant, who had come up with Mr. Vane, but left his heart at Willoughby. James Burdock had for some time been ruminating, and his conclusion was, that his mistress, Miss Mabel, (as by force of habit he called her,) was not treated as she deserved.

Burdock had been imported into Mr. Vane's family by Mabel. He had carried her in his arms when she was a child; he had held her upon a donkey when she was a little girl; and when she became a woman, it was he who taught her to stand close to her horse, and give him her foot, and spring while he lifted her steadily but strongly into her saddle; and when there it was he who had instructed her that a horse was not a machine, that galloping tires it in time, and that galloping it on the hard road hammers it to pieces. "I taught the girl," thought James within himself.

This honest, silver-haired old fellow seemed so ridiculous to Colander, the smooth, supercilious Londoner, that he deigned sometimes to converse with James, in order to quiz him. This very morning they had had a conversation.

"Poor Miss Mabel! dear heart. A twelve month married, and nigh six months of it a widow, or next door."

"We write to her, James, and entertain her replies, which are at considerable length."

"Ay, but we don't read 'em!" said James, with an uneasy glance at the tray.

"Invariably, at our leisure; meantime we make ourselves happy amongst the wits and the sirens."

"And she do make others happy among the poor and the ailing."

"Which shows," said Colander, superciliously, "the difference of tastes."

Burdock, whose eye had never been off his mistress's handwriting, at last took it up and said, "Master Colander, do, if ye please, sir, take this into master's dressing room, do now."

Colander looked down on the missive with dilating eye. "Not a bill, James Burdock," said he, reproachfully.

"A bill! bless ye, no. A letter from missus."

No; the dog would not take it in to his master, and poor James, with a sigh, replaced it in the tray.

This James Burdock, then, was left in charge of the hall by Colander, and it so happened that the change was hardly effected before a hurried knocking came to the street door.

"Ay, ay!" grumbled Burdock, "I thought it would not be long. London for knocking and ringing all day, and ringing and knocking all night." He opened the door reluctantly and suspiciously, and in darted a lady, whose features were concealed by a hood. She glided across the hall, as if she was making for some point, and old James shuffled after her, crying, "Stop, stop! young woman. What is your name, young wo man?"

"Why, James Burdock," cried the lady, removing her hood, "have you forgotten your mistress?"

"Mistress? Why, Miss Mabel, I ask your pardon, madam — here John, Margery!"

"Hush!" cried Mrs. Vane.

"But where are your trunks, miss? And where's the coach, and Darby and Joan? To think of their drawing you all the way here! I'll have 'em into your room directly, ma'am. Miss, you've come just in time."

"What a dear, good, stupid old thing you are, James! Where is Ernest — Mr. Vane? James, is he well and happy? I want to surprise him."

"Yes, ma'am," said James, looking down.

"I left the stupid old coach at Islington, James. The something — pin was loose, or I don't know what. Could I wait two hours there? So I came on by myself; you wicked old man, you let me talk, and don't tell me how he is."

"Master is main well, ma'am, and thank you," said old Burdock, confused and uneasy.

"But is he happy? Of course he is. Are we not to meet to-day after six months? Ah! but never mind, they *are* gone by."

"Lord bless her!" thought the faithful old fellow. "If sitting down and crying could help her, I wouldn't be long."

By this time they were in the banqueting room, and at the preparations there Mabel gave a start; she then colored. "O, he has invited his friends to make acquaintance. I had rather we had been alone all this day and to-morrow. But he must not know that. No; *his* friends are *my* friends, and shall be too," thought the country wife. She then glanced with some misgiving at her travelling attire, and wished she had brought *one* trunk with her.

"James," said she, "where is my room? And mind, I forbid you to tell a soul I am come."

"Your room, Miss Mabel?"

"Well, any room where there is looking glass and water."

She then went to a door which opened in fact

on a short passage leading to a room occupied by Mr. Vane himself.

"No, no!" cried James. "That is master's room."

"Well, is not master's room mistress's room, old man? But stay; is he there?"

"No ma'am; he is in the garden with a power of fine folks."

"They shall not see me till I have made myself a little more decent," said the young beauty, who knew at bottom how little comparatively the color of her dress could affect her appearance, and she opened Mr. Vane's door and glided in.

Burdock's first determination was, in spite of her injunction, to tell Colander; but on reflection he argued, "And then what will they do? They will put their heads together, and deceive us some other way. No!" thought James, with a touch of spite, "we shall see how they will all look." He argued, also, that at sight of his beautiful wife, his master must come to his senses, and the Colander faction be defeated; and, perhaps, by the mercy of Providence, Colander himself turned off.

Whilst thus ruminating, a thundering knock at the door almost knocked him off his legs. "There ye go again," said he, and went angrily to the door. This time it was Hunsdon, who was in a desperate hurry to see his master.

"Where is Sir Charles Pomander, my honest fellow?" said he.

"In the garden, my Jack-a-dandy!" said Burdock, furiously.

("Honest fellow," among servants, implies some moral inferiority.)

Into the garden went Hunsdon. His master — all whose senses were playing sentinel — saw him, and left the company to meet him.

"She is in the house, sir."

"Good! Go — vanish!"

Sir Charles looked into the banquet room; the haunch was being placed on the table. He returned with the information. He burned to bring husband and wife together. He counted each second lost that postponed this (to him) thrilling joy. O, how happy he was! — happier than the serpent, when he saw Eve's white teeth strike into the apple!

"Shall we pay respect to this haunch, Mr. Quin?" said Vane, gayly.

"If you please, sir," said Quin, gravely.

Colander ran down a by path with an immense bouquet, which he arranged for Mrs. Woffington in a vase at Mr. Vane's left hand. He then threw open the windows, which were on the French plan, and shut within a foot of the lawn.

The musicians in the arbor struck up, and the company, led by Mr. Vane and Mrs. Woffington, entered the room. And a charming room it was! — light, lofty, and large — adorned in the French way, with white and gold. The table was an exact oval, and at it every body could hear what any one said; an excellent arrangement where ideaed guests only are admitted — which is another excellent arrangement, though I see people don't think so.

The repast was luxurious and elegant. There was no profusion of unmeaning dishes; each was a *bonne-bouche* — an undeniable delicacy. The glass was beautiful, the plates silver; the flowers rose like walls from the table; the plate massive and glorious; rose water in the hand glasses; music crept in from the garden, deliciously subdued into what seemed a natural sound. A broad stream of southern sun gushed in fiery gold through the open window, and, like a red-hot rainbow, danced through the stained glass above it. Existence was a thing to bask in — in such a place, and so happy an hour!

The guests were Quin, Mrs. Clive, Mr. Cibber, Sir Charles Pomander, Mrs. Woffington, and Messrs. Soaper and Snarl, critics of the day. This pair, with wonderful sagacity, had arrived from the street as the haunch came from the kitchen. Good humor reigned; some cuts passed, but as the parties professed wit, they gave and took.

Quin carved the haunch, and was happy; Soaper and Snarl eating the same, and drinking Tokay, were mellowed and mitigated into human flesh. Mr. Vane and Mrs. Woffington were happy; he, because his conscience was asleep; and she, because she felt nothing now could shake her hold of him. Sir Charles was in a sort of mental chuckle. His head burned, his bones ached; but he was in a sort of nervous delight.

"Where is she?" thought he. "What will she do? Will she send her maid with a note? How blue he will look! Or, will she come herself? She is a country wife; there must be a scene. O, why doesn't she come into this room? She must know we are here! Is she watching some where?" His brain became puzzled, and his senses were sharpened to a point; he was all eye, ear, and expectation; and this was why he was the only one to hear a very slight sound behind the door we have mentioned, and next to perceive a lady's glove lying close to that door. Mabel had dropped it in her retreat. Putting this and that together, he was led to hope and believe she was there, making her toilet, perhaps, and her arrival at present unknown.

"Do you expect no one else?" said he, with feigned carelessness, to Mr. Vane.

"No," said Mr. Vane, with real carelessness.

"It must be so! What fortune!" thought Pomander.

Soaper. — Mr. Cibber looks no older than he did five years ago.

Snarl. — There was no room on his face for a fresh wrinkle.

Soaper. — He! he! Nay, Mr. Snarl; Mr. Cibber is like old port; the more ancient he grows, the more delicious his perfume.

SNARL. — And the crustier he gets.

CLIVE. — Mr. Vane, you should always separate those two. Snarl, by himself, is just supportable; but when Soaper paves the way with his hypocritical praise, the pair are too much; they are a two-edged sword.

WOFFINGTON. — Wanting nothing but polish and point.

VANE. — Gentlemen, we abandon your neighbor, Mr. Quin, to you.

QUIN. — They know better. If they don't keep a civil tongue in their heads, no fat goes from here to them.

CIBBER. — Ah, Mr. Vane, this room is delightful; but it makes me sad. I knew this house in Lord Longueville's time; an unrivalled gallant, Peggy. You may just remember him, Sir Charles.

POMANDER, (with his eye on a certain door.) — Yes, yes; a gouty old fellow.

Cibber fired up. "I wish you may ever be like him. O, the beauty, the wit, the *petits-soupers* that used to be here! Longueville was a great creature, Mr. Vane. I have known him entertain a fine lady in this room, while her rival was fretting and fuming on the other side of that door."

"Ah, indeed!" said Sir Charles.

"More shame for him," said Mr. Vane.

Here was luck! Pomander seized this opportunity of turning the conversation to his object. With a malicious twinkle in his eye, he inquired of Mr. Cibber what made him fancy the house had lost its virtue in Mr. Vane's hands.

"Because," said Cibber, peevishly, "you all want the true *savoir faire* nowadays, because there is no *juste milieu,* young gentlemen. The young dogs of the day are all either unprincipled heathen, like yourself, or Amadises, like our worthy host." The old gentleman's face and manners were like those of a patriarch, regretting the general decay of virtue, not the imaginary diminution of a single vice. He concluded, with a sigh, that "The true *preux des dames* went out with the full periwig; stap my vitals!"

"A bit of fat, Mr. Cibber?" said Quin, whose jokes were not polished.

"Jemmy, thou art a brute," was the reply.

"You refuse, sir?" said Quin, sternly.

"No, sir!" said Cibber, with dignity; "I accept."

Pomander's eye was ever on the door.

"The old are so unjust to the young," said he. "You pretend that the deluge washed away iniquity, and that a rake is a fossil. What," said he, leaning as it were on every word, "if I bet you a cool hundred, that Vane has a petticoat in that room, and that Mrs. Woffington shall unearth her?"

The malicious dog thought this was the surest way to effect a dramatic exposure; because, if Peggy found Mabel to all appearances concealed, Peggy would scold her, and betray herself.

"Pomander!" cried Vane, in great heat; then checking himself, he said coolly, "But you all know Pomander."

"None of you," replied that gentleman. "Bring a chair, sir," said he, authoritatively to a servant; who, of course, obeyed.

Mrs. Clive looked at him, and thought, "There is something in this!"

"It is for the lady," said he coolly. Then, leaning over the table, he said to Mrs. Woffington, with an impudent affectation of friendly understanding, "I ran her to earth in this house not ten minutes ago. Of course, I don't know who she is! But," smacking his lips, "a rustic

Amaryllis, breathing all May-buds and Meadow-sweet."

"Have her out, Peggy!" shouted Cibber. "I know the run — there's the covert! Hark forward! Ha! ha! ha!"

Mr. Vane rose, and with a sternness that brought the old beau up with a run, he said, "Mr. Cibber, age and infirmity are privileged; but for you, Sir Charles ——"

"Don't be angry," interposed Mrs. Woffington, whose terror was lest he should quarrel with so practised a swordsman. "Don't you see it is a jest! and, as might be expected from poor Sir Charles, a very sorry one."

"A jest!" said Vane, white with rage. "Let it go no farther, or it will be earnest!"

Mrs. Woffington placed her hand on his shoulder, and at that touch he instantly yielded, and sat down.

It was at this moment, when Sir Charles found himself for the present baffled — for he could no longer press his point, and search that room; when the attention of all was drawn to a dispute, which, for a moment, had looked like a quarrel; whilst Mrs. Woffington's hand still lingered, as only a woman's hand can linger in leaving the shoulder of the man she loves; it was at this moment, the door opened of its own accord, and a most beautiful woman stood, with a light step, upon the threshold!

Nobody's back was to her, except Mr. Vane's. Every eye, but his, was spell-bound upon her.

Mrs. Woffington withdrew her hand, as if a scorpion had touched her.

A stupor of astonishment fell on them all.

Mr. Vane, seeing the direction of all their eyes, slued himself round in his chair into a most awkward position, and when he saw the lady, he was utterly dumbfounded! But she, as soon as he turned his face her way, glided up to him with a little half sigh, half cry of joy, and taking him round the neck, kissed him deliciously, while every eye at the table met every other eye in turn. One or two of the men rose; for the lady's beauty was as worthy of homage as her appearing was marvellous.

Mrs. Woffington, too astonished for emotion to take any definite shape, said, in what seemed an ordinary tone, "Who is this lady?"

"I am his wife, madam," said Mabel, in the

voice of a skylark, and smiling friendly on the questioner.

"It is my wife!" said Vane, like a speaking machine; he was scarcely in a conscious state. "It is my wife!" he repeated mechanically.

The words were no sooner out of Mabel's mouth than two servants, who had never heard of Mrs. Vane before, hastened to place on Mr. Vane's right hand the chair Pomander had provided; a plate and napkin were there in a twinkling, and the wife modestly, but as a matter of course, courtesied low, with an air of welcome to all her guests, and then glided into the seat her servants obsequiously placed for her.

The whole thing did not take half a minute!

CHAPTER XI.

Mr. Vane, besides being a rich, was a magnificent man; when his features were in repose their beauty had a wise and stately character. Soaper and Snarl had admired, and bitterly envied him. At the present moment no one of his guests envied him — they began to realize his position. And he, a huge wheel of shame and remorse, began to turn and whirr before his eyes. He sat between two European beauties; and pale and red by turns, shunned the eyes of both, and looked down at his plate in a cold sweat of humiliation, mortification, and shame.

The iron passed through Mrs. Woffington's soul. So! this was a villain, too; the greatest villain of all — a hypocrite! She turned very faint, but she was under an enemy's eye, and under a rival's; the thought drove the blood back from her heart, and with a mighty effort she was Woffington again. Hitherto her *liaison* with Mr. Vane had called up the better part of her nature, and perhaps our reader has been taking her for a good woman ; but now all her dregs were stirred to the surface. The mortified actress gulled by a novice, the wronged and insulted woman, had but two thoughts ; to defeat her rival — to be revenged on her false lover. More than one sharp spasm passed over her features before she could master them, and then she became smiles above, wormwood and red-hot steel below — all in less than half a minute.

As for the others, looks of keen intelligence passed between them, and they watched with burning interest for the *dénouement.* That interest was stronger than their sense of the comicality of all this, (for the humorous view of what passes before our eyes, comes upon cool reflection, not often at the time.)

Sir Charles, indeed, who had foreseen some of this, wore a demure look, belied by his glittering eye. He offered Cibber snuff, and the two satirical animals grinned over the snuffbox like a malicious old ape and a mischievous young monkey.

The new comer was charming ; she was above the middle height, of a full, though graceful figure, her abundant, glossy, bright brown hair glittered here and there like gold in the light; she had a snowy brow, eyes of the profoundest blue, a cheek like a peach, and a face beaming candor and goodness; the character of her countenance resembled "the Queen of the May," in Mr. Leslie's famous picture, more than any face of our day I can call to mind.

"You are not angry with me for this silly trick?" said she, with some misgiving. "After all I am only two hours before my time; you know, dearest, I said four in my letter — did I not?"

Vane stammered. What could he say?

"And you have had three days to prepare you, for I wrote, like a good wife, to ask leave before starting; but he never so much as answered my letter, madam." (This she addressed to Mrs. Woffington, who smiled by main force.)

"Why," stammered Vane, "could you doubt? I — I —"

"No! Silence was consent, was it not? But I beg your pardon, ladies and gentlemen, I hope you will forgive me. It is six months since I saw him — so you understand — I warrant me you did not look for me so soon, ladies?"

"Some of us did not look for you at all, madam," said Mrs. Woffington.

"What, Ernest did not tell you he expected me?"

"No! He told us this banquet was in honor of a lady's first visit to his house, but none of us imagined that lady to be his wife."

Vane began to writhe under that terrible tongue, whose point hitherto had ever been turned away from him.

"He intended to steal a march on us," said Pomander, dryly; "and with your help, we steal one on him;" and he smiled maliciously on Mrs. Woffington.

"But, madam," said Mr. Quin, "the moment you did arrive, I kept sacred for you a bit of the fat; for which, I am sure, you must be ready. Pass her plate!"

"Not at present, Mr. Quin," said Mr. Vane, hastily. "She is about to retire and change her travelling dress."

"Yes, dear; but you forget, I am a stranger to your friends. Will you not introduce me to them first?"

"No, no!" cried Vane, in trepidation. "It is not usual to introduce in the *beau monde*."

"We always introduce ourselves," rejoined Mrs. Woffington; and she rose slowly, with her eye on Vane. He cast a look of abject entreaty on her; but there was no pity in that curling lip and awful eye. He closed his own eyes, and waited for the blow. Sir Charles threw himself back in his chair, and chuckling, prepared for the explosion. Mrs. Woffington saw him, and cast on him a look of ineffable scorn; and then she held the whole company fluttering a long while. At length, "The Honorable Mrs. Quickly, madam," said she, indicating Mrs. Clive.

This turn took them all by surprise. Pomander bit his lip.

"Sir John Brute ——"

"Falstaff," cried Quin; "hang it."

"Sir John Brute Falstaff," resumed Mrs. Woffington. "We call him, for brevity, Brute."

Vane drew a long breath. "Your neighbor is Lord Foppington; a butterfly of some standing, and a little gouty."

"Sir Charles Pomander."

"O!" cried Mrs. Vane. "It is the good gentleman who helped us out of the slough near Huntingdon. Ernest, if it had not been for this gentleman, I should not have had the pleasure of being here now." And she beamed on the good Pomander.

Mr. Vane did not rise and embrace Sir Charles.

"All the company thanks the good Sir Charles," said Cibber, bowing.

"I see it in all their faces," said the good Sir Charles, dryly.

Mrs. Woffington continued: "Mr. Soaper, Mr. Snarl; gentlemen who would butter and slice up their own fathers!"

"Bless me!" cried Mrs. Vane, faintly.

"Critics!" And she dropped, as it were, the word dryly, with a sweet smile, into Mabel's plate.

Mrs. Vane was relieved; she had apprehended cannibals. London they had told her was full of curiosities.

"But yourself, madam?"

"I am the Lady Betty Modish; at your service."

A four inch grin went round the table. The dramatical old rascal, Cibber, began now to look at it as a bit of genteel comedy, and slipped out his note book under the table. Pomander cursed her ready wit, which had disappointed him of his catastrophe. Vane wrote on a slip of paper, "Pity and respect the innocent!" and passed it to Mrs. Woffington. He could not have done a more superfluous or injudicious thing.

"And now, Ernest," cried Mabel, "for the news from Willoughby."

Vane stopped her in dismay. He felt how many satirical eyes and ears were upon him and his wife. "Pray go and change your dress first, Mabel," cried he, fully determined that on her return she should not find the present party there.

Mrs. Vane cast an imploring look on Mrs. Woffington. "My things are not come," said she. "And, Lady Betty, I had so much to tell him, and to be sent away;" and the deep blue eyes began to fill.

Now, Mrs. Woffington was determined that this lady, who she saw was simple, should disgust her husband, by talking twaddle before a band of satirists. So she said warmly, "It is not fair on us. Pray, madam, your budget of country news. Clouted cream so seldom comes to London quite fresh."

"There, you see, Ernest," said the unsuspicious soul. "First, you must know that Gray Gillian is turned out for a brood mare, so old George won't let me ride her; old servants are such tyrants, my lady. And my Barbary hen has laid two eggs; Heaven knows the trouble we had to bring her to it. And Dame Best, that is my husband's old nurse, Mrs. Quickly, has had soup and pudding from the hall every day, and once she went so far as to say it wasn't altogether a bad pudding. She is not a very grateful woman, in a general way, poor thing! I made it with these hands."

Vane writhed.

"Happy pudding!" observed Mr. Cibber.

"Is this mockery, sir?" cried Vane, with a sudden burst of irritation.

"No, sir; it is gallantry," replied Cibber, with perfect coolness.

"Will you hear a little music in the garden?" said Vane to Mrs. Woffington, pooh-poohing his wife's news.

"Not till I hear the end of Dame Bess."

"Best, my lady."

"Dame Best interests *me*, Mr. Vane."

"Ay! and Ernest is very fond of her, too, when he is at home. She is in her nice new cottage, dear; but she misses the draughts that were in her old one — they were like old friends. 'The only ones I have, I'm thinking,' said the dear, cross old thing; and there stood I, on her floor, with a flannel petticoat in both hands, that I had made for her, and ruined my finger. Look else, my Lord Foppington!" She extended a hand the color of cream.

"Permit me, madam?" taking out his glasses, with which he inspected her finger; and gravely announced to the company, "The laceration is, in fact, discernible. May I be permitted, madam," added he, "to kiss this fair hand, which I should never have suspected of having ever made itself half so useful?"

"Ay, my lord!" said she, coloring slightly, "you shall, because you are so old; but I don't say for a young gentleman, unless it was the one that belongs to me; and he does not ask me."

"My dear Mabel, pray remember we are not at Willoughby."

"I see we are not, Ernest." And the dove-like eyes filled brimful; and all her innocent prattle was put an end to.

"What brutes men are!" thought Mrs. Woffington. "They are not worthy even of a fool like this."

Mr. Vane once more pressed her to hear a little music in the garden; and this time she consented. Mr. Vane was far from being unmoved by his wife's arrival, and her true affection. But she worried him; he was anxious, above all things, to escape from his present position, and separate the rival queens; and this was the only way he could see to do it. He whispered Mabel, and bade her, somewhat peremptorily, rest herself for an hour after her journey, and he entered the garden with Mrs. Woffington.

Now, the other gentlemen admired Mrs. Vane the most. She was new. She was as lovely, in her way, as Peggy; and it was the young May-morn beauty of the country. They forgave her simplicity, and even her goodness, on account of her beauty; men are not severe judges of beautiful women. They all solicited her to come with them, and be the queen of the garden. But the good wife was obedient. Her lord had told her she was fatigued; so she said she was tired.

"Mr. Vane's garden will lack its sweetest and fairest flower, madam," cried Cibber, "if we leave you here."

"Nay, my lord, there are fairer than I."

"Poor Quin!" cried Kitty Clive; "to have to leave the alderman's walk for the garden walk."

"All I regret," said the honest glutton, stoutly, "is that I go without carving for Mrs. Vane."

"You are very good, Sir John; I will be more troublesome to you at supper time."

When they were all gone, she couldn't help sighing. It almost seemed as if every body was kinder to her than he whose kindness alone she valued. "And he must take Lady Betty's hand instead of mine," thought she. "But that is good breeding, I suppose. I wish there was no such thing; we are very happy without it in Shropshire." Then this poor little soul was ashamed of herself, and took herself to task. "Poor Ernest," said she, pitying the wrong-doer, like a woman, "he was not pleased to be so taken by surprise. No wonder; they are so ceremonious in London. How good of him not to be angry!" Then she sighed; her heart had received a damp. His voice seemed changed, and he did not meet her eyes with the look he wore at Willoughby. She looked timidly into the garden. She saw the gay colors of beaux, as well as of belles — for in these days broadcloth had not displaced silk and velvet — glancing and shining among the trees; and she sighed, but presently brightening up a little, she said, "I will go and see that the coffee is hot and clear, and the chocolate well mixed for them." The poor child wanted to do something to please her husband. Before she could carry out this act of domestic virtue, her attention was drawn to a strife of tongues in the hall. She opened the folding doors, and there was a fine gentleman obstructing the entrance of a sombre, rusty figure, with a portfolio and a manuscript under each arm.

The fine gentleman was Colander. The seedy personage was the eternal Triplet, come to make hay with his five-foot rule while the sun shone. Colander had opened the door to him, and he had shot into the hall. The major domo obstructed the farther entrance of such a coat.

"I tell you my master is not at home," remonstrated the major domo.

"How can you say so," cried Mrs. Vane, in surprise, "when you know he is in the garden?"

"Simpleton!" thought Colander.

"Show the gentleman in."

"Gentleman!" muttered Colander.

Triplet thanked her for her condescension; he would wait for Mr. Vane in the hall. "I came by appointment, madam; this is the only excuse for the importunity you have just witnessed."

Hearing this, Mrs. Vane dismissed Colander to inform his master. Colander bowed loftily, and walked into the servants' hall without deigning to take the last proposition into consideration.

"Come in here, sir," said Mabel; "Mr. Vane will come as soon as he can leave his company." Triplet entered in a series of obsequious jerks. "Sit down and rest you, sir." And Mrs. Vane seated herself at the table, and motioned with her white hand to Triplet to sit beside her.

Triplet bowed, and sat on the edge of a chair, and smirked and dropped his portfolio, and instantly begged Mrs. Vane's pardon; in taking it up, he let fall his manuscript, and was again confused; but in the middle of some superfluous and absurd excuse his eye fell on the haunch; it straightway dilated to an enormous size, and he became suddenly silent and absorbed in contemplation.

"You look sadly tired, sir."

"Why, yes, madam. It is a long way from Lambeth Walk, and it is passing hot, madam." He took his handkerchief out, and was about to wipe his brow, but returned it hastily to his pocket. "I beg your pardon, madam," said Triplet, whose ideas of breeding, though speculative, were severe, "I forgot myself."

Mabel looked at him, and colored, and slightly hesitated. At last she said, "I'll be bound you came in such a hurry you forgot — you musn't be angry with me — to have your dinner first?"

For Triplet looked like an absurd wolf — all benevolence and starvation!

"What divine intelligence!" thought Trip. "How strange, madam," cried he, "you have hit it! This accounts, at once, for a craving I feel. Now you remind me, I recollect carving for others, I did forget to remember myself. Not that I need have forgot it to-day, madam; but being used to forget it, I did not remember not to forget it to-day, madam, that was all." And the author of this intelligent account smiled, very, very, very absurdly.

She poured him out a glass of wine. He rose and bowed; but peremptorily refused it, with his tongue — his eye drank it.

"But you must," persisted this hospitable lady.

"But, madam, consider I am not entitled to — Nectar, as I am a man!"

The white hand was filling his plate with partridge pie: "But, madam, you don't consider how you overwhelm me with your — Ambrosia, as I am a poet!"

"I am sorry Mr. Vane should keep you waiting."

"By no means, madam; it is very fortunate — I mean it procures me the pleasure of —" (here articulation became obstructed) "your society, madam. Besides, the servants of the Muse are used to waiting. What we are not used to is" (here the white hand filled his glass) "being waited upon by Hebe and the Twelve Graces, whose health I have the honor ——" (Deglutition.)

"A poet!" cried Mabel; "O, I am so glad! Little did I think ever to see a living poet! Dear heart! I should not have known, if you had not told me. Sir, I love poetry!"

"It is in your face, madam." Triplet instantly whipped out his manuscript, put a plate on one corner of it, and a decanter on the other, and begged her opinion of this trifle, composed, said he, "in honor of a lady Mr. Vane entertains to-day."

"O," said Mrs. Vane, and colored with pleasure. How ungrateful she had been! Here was an attention! — For, of course, she never doubted that the verses were in honor of her arrival.

"'Bright being ——'"

sang out Triplet.

"Nay, sir," said Mabel; "I think I know the lady, and it would be hardly proper of me ——"

"O madam!" said Triplet, solemnly; "strictly correct, madam!" And he spread his hand out over his bosom. "Strictly! — 'Blunderbuss' (my poetical name, madam) never stooped to the taste of the town.

'Bright being, thou ——'"

"But you must have another glass of wine first, and a slice of the haunch."

"With alacrity, madam." He laid in a fresh stock of provisions.

Strange it was, to see them side by side! *he*, a Don Quixote, with cordage instead of lines in his mahogany face, and clothes hanging upon him: *she*, smooth, duck-like, delicious, and bright as an opening rose fresh with dew!

She watched him kindly, archly, and demurely, and still plied him, country-wise, with every mortal thing on the table.

But the poet was not a boa constrictor, and even a boa constrictor has an end. Hunger satisfied, his next strongest feeling, simple vanity, remained to be contented. As the last morsel went in out came, —

"'Bright being, thou whose ra ——'"

"No! no!" said she, who fancied herself (and not without reason) the bright being. "Mr. Vane intended them for a surprise."

"As you please, madam;" and the disappointed bore sighed. "But you would have liked them, for the theme inspired me. The kindest, the most generous of women! Don't you agree with me, madam?"

Mabel Vane opened her eyes. "Hardly, sir," laughed she.

"If you knew her as I do!"

"I ought to know her better, sir."

"Ay, indeed! Well, madam, now her kindness to me, for instance — a poor devil like me! The expression, I trust, is not disagreeable to you, madam? If so, forgive me, and consider it withdrawn."

"La, sir! civility is so cheap, if you go to that."

"Civility, ma'am? Why, she has saved me from despair — from starvation, perhaps."

"Poor thing! Well, indeed, sir, you looked — you looked — what a shame! and you a poet!"

"From an epitaph to an epic, madam."

At this moment a figure looked in upon them from the garden, but retreated unobserved. It was Sir Charles Pomander, who had slipped away with the heartless and malicious intention of exposing the husband to the wife, and profiting by her indignation and despair. Seeing Triplet, he made an extemporaneous calculation that so infernal a chatterbox could not be ten minutes in her company without telling her every thing — and this would serve his turn very well. He therefore postposed his purpose, and strolled away to a short distance.

Triplet justified the baronet's opinion. Without any sort of sequency, he now informed Mrs. Vane that the benevolent lady was to sit to him for her portrait.

Here was a new attention of Ernest's. How good he was! and how wicked and ungrateful she!

"What! are you a painter too?" she inquired.

"From a house front to an historical composi tion, madam."

"O, what a clever man! And so Ernest com missioned you to paint a portrait?"

"No, madam; for that I am indebted to the lady herself."

"The lady herself?"

"Yes, madam; and I expected to find her here. Will you add to your kindness by informing me whether she has arrived? Or she is gone ——"

"Who, sir? (O dear! not my portrait! O Ernest!)"

"Who, madam?" cried Triplet. "Why, Mrs. Woffington."

"She is not here," said Mrs. Vane, who remembered all the names perfectly well. "There is one charming lady among our guests; her face took me in a moment; but she is a titled lady: there is no Mrs. Woffington amongst them."

"Strange!" replied Triplet. "She was to be here; and in fact that is why I expedited these lines in her honor."

"In *her* honor, sir?"

"Yes, madam. Allow me: —

'Bright being! thou whose radiant brow ——'"

"No, no. I don't care to hear them now; for I don't know the lady."

"Well, madam — but at least you have seen her act?"

"Act! You don't mean all this is for an actress?"

"*An* actress? *The* actress! And you have never seen her act? What a pleasure you have to come! To see her act is a privilege; but to act with her as *I* once did! But she does not remember that, nor shall I remind her, madam," said Triplet, sternly. "On that occasion I was hissed, owing to circumstances, which, for the credit of our common nature, I suppress."

"What! are you an actor too? You are every thing."

"And it was in a farce of my own, madam, which, by the strangest combination of accidents, was damned."

"A play writer? O, what clever men there are in the world—in London, at least! He is a play writer too. I wonder my husband comes not. Does Mr. Vane—does Mr. Vane admire this actress?" said she, suddenly.

"Mr. Vane, madam, is a gentleman of taste," said he, pompously.

"Well, sir," said the lady, languidly, "she is not here." Triplet took the hint, and rose. "Good by," said she, sweetly; "and thank you kindly for your company, Mr.—Mr. ——"

"Triplet, madam—James Triplet, of 10, Hercules Buildings, Lambeth. Occasional verses, odes, epithalamia, elegies, dedications, squibs, impromptus, and hymns, executed with spirit, punctuality, and secrecy. Portraits painted, and instruction in declamation—sacred, profane, and dramatic. The card, madam," (and he drew it as doth a theatrical fop his rapier,) "of him, who, to all these qualifications, adds a prouder still — that of being,

"Madam,

"Your humble, devoted, and grateful servant,

"JAMES TRIPLET."

He bowed in a line from his right shoulder to his left toe, and moved off. But Triplet could not go all at one time out of such company; he was given to return in real life, he had played this trick so often on the stage. He came back exuberant with gratitude.

"The fact is, madam," said he, "strange as it may appear to you, a kind hand has not so often been held out to me, that I should forget it, especially when that hand is so fair and gracious. May I be permitted, madam — you will impute it to gratitude, rather than audacity — I — I — " (whimper) — "Madam," (with sudden severity,) "I am gone!"

These last words he pronounced with the right arm at an angle of forty-five degrees, and the fingers pointing horizontally. The stage had taught him this grace also. In his day an actor who had three words to say, such as, "My lord's carriage is waiting," came on the stage with the right arm thus elevated, delivered his message in the tone of a falling dynasty, wheeled like a soldier, and retired with the left arm pointing to the sky, and the right extended behind him like a setter's tail.

Left to herself, Mabel was uneasy. "Ernest is so warm-hearted." This was the way she put it even to herself. He admired her acting, and wished to pay her a compliment. "What if I carried him the verses?" She thought she should surely please him by showing she was not the least jealous or doubtful of him. The poor child wanted so to win a kind look from her husband; but ere she could reach the window, Sir Charles Pomander had entered it.

Now, Sir Charles was naturally welcome to Mrs. Vane; for all she knew of him was, that he had helped her on the road to her husband.

Pomander. — What, madam! all alone here, as in Shropshire?

Mabel. — For the moment, sir.

Pomander. — Force of habit. A husband with a wife in Shropshire is so like a bachelor.

MABEL. — Sir!

POMANDER. — And our excellent Ernest is such a favorite!

MABEL. — No wonder, sir.

POMANDER. — Few can so pass from the larva state of country squire to the butterfly nature of beau.

MABEL. — Yes, (sadly,) I find him changed.

POMANDER. — Changed! Transformed. He is now the prop of the "Cocoa Tree," the star of Ranelagh, the Lauzun of the greenroom.

MABEL. — The greenroom! Where is that? You mean kindly, sir; but you make me unhappy.

POMANDER. — The greenroom, my dear madam, is the bower where houris put off their wings, and goddesses become dowdies; where Lady Macbeth weeps over her lapdog, dead from repletion; and Belvidera soothes her broken heart with a dozen of oysters. In a word, it is the place where actors and actresses become men and women, and act their own parts with skill, instead of a poet's, clumsily.

MABEL. — Actors! actresses! Does Mr. Vane frequent such ——

POMANDER. — He has earned in six months a reputation many a fine gentleman would give his ears for. Not a scandalous journal his initials have not figured in; not an actress of reputation gossip has not given him for a conquest.

"How dare you say this to me?" cried Mrs. Vane, with a sudden flash of indignation, and then the tears streamed over her lovely cheeks; and even a Pomander might have forborne to torture her so; but Sir Charles had no mercy.

"You would be sure to learn it," said he, "and with malicious additions. It is better to hear the truth from a friend."

"A friend? He is no friend to a house who calumniates the husband to the wife. Is it the part of a friend to distort dear Ernest's kindliness and gayety into ill morals? to pervert his love of poetry and plays into an unworthy attachment to actors and —— O!" and the tears would come. But she dried them, for now she hated this man; with all the little power of hatred she had she detested him. "Do you suppose I did not know Mrs. Woffington was to come to us to-day?" cried she, struggling passionately against her own fears and Sir Charles's innuendoes.

"What!" cried he; "you recognized her? You detected the actress of all work under the airs of Lady Betty Modish!"

"Lady Betty Modish!" cried Mabel: "that good, beautiful face!"

"Ah!" cried Sir Charles, "I see you did not. Well, Lady Betty was Mrs. Woffington!"

"Whom my husband, I know, had invited here to present her with these verses, which I shall take him for her;" and her poor little lip trembled. "Had the visit been in any other character, as you are so base, so cruel as to insin uate, (what have I done to you that you kill me so, you wicked gentleman?) would he have chosen the day of my arrival?"

"Not if he knew you were coming," was the cool reply.

"And he did know; I wrote to him."

"Indeed!" said Pomander, fairly puzzled.

Mrs. Vane caught sight of her handwriting on the tray, and darted to it, and seized her letter, and said, triumphantly, —

"My last letter, written upon the road; see!"

Sir Charles took it with surprise, but turning it in his hand, a cool satirical smile came to his face. He handed it back, and said coldly, —

"Read me the passage, madam, on which you argue."

Poor Mrs. Vane turned the letter in her hand, and her eye became instantly glazed; the seal was unbroken! She gave a sharp cry of agony, like a wounded deer. She saw Pomander no longer; she was alone with her great anguish. "I had but my husband and my God in the world," cried she. "My mother is gone. My God, have pity on me! my husband does not love me."

The cold villain was startled at the mighty storm his mean hand had raised. This creature had not only more feeling, but more passion than a hundred libertines. He muttered some villain's commonplaces; while this unhappy young lady raised her hands to heaven, and sobbed in a way very terrible to any manly heart.

"He is unworthy you," muttered Pomander. "He has forfeited your love; he has left you nothing but revenge. Be comforted. Let me, who have learned already to adore you —— "

"So," cried she, turning on him in a moment, (for on some points, woman's instinct is the lightning of wisdom,) "this, sir, was your object? I may no longer hold a place in my husband's heart; but I am mistress of his house. Leave it, sir! and never return to it whilst I live."

Sir Charles, again discomfited, bowed reverentially. "Your wish shall ever be respected by me, madam! But here they come. Use the right of a wife. Conceal yourself in that high chair. See! I turn it, so that they cannot see you. At least, you will find I have but told you the truth."

"No!" cried Mabel, violently. "I will not spy upon my husband at the dictation of his treacherous friend."

Sir Charles vanished. He was no sooner gone than Mrs. Vane crouched, trembling, and writhing with jealousy, in the large, high-backed chair. She heard her husband and the *soi-disant* Lady Betty Modish enter. During their absence Mrs. Woffington had, doubtless, been playing her cards with art; for it appeared that a reconciliation was now taking place. The lady, however, was still cool and distant. It was poor Mabel's fate to hear these words : " You must permit me to go alone, Mr. Vane. I insist upon leaving this house alone."

On this he whispered to her.

She answered, " You are not justified."

" I can explain all," was his reply. " I am ready to renounce credit, character, all the world for you."

They passed out of the room before the unhappy listener could recover the numbing influence of these deadly words.

But the next moment she started wildly up, and cried, as one drowning cries vaguely for help, " Ernest ! O no — no ! you cannot use me so ! Ernest — husband ! O mother ! mother ! "

She rose, and would have made for the door, but nature had been too cruelly tried. At the first step she could no longer see any thing ; and the next moment swooning dead away, she fell back insensible, with her head and shoulders resting on the chair.

CHAPTER XII.

Mr. Vane was putting Mrs. Woffington into her chair, when he thought he heard his name cried. He bade that lady a mournful farewell, and stepped back into his own hall. He had no sooner done so, than he heard a voice, the accent of which alarmed him, though he distinguished no word. He hastily crossed the hall, and flew into the banquet room. Coming rapidly in at the folding doors, he almost fell over his wife, lying insensible, half upon the floor, and half upon the chair. When he saw her pale and motionless, a terrible misgiving seized him; he fell on his knees.

"Mabel, Mabel!" cried he, "my love! my innocent wife! O God! what have I done? Perhaps it is the fatigue—perhaps she has fainted."

"No, it is not the fatigue!" screamed a voice near him. It was old James Burdock, who, with his white hair streaming, and his eye gleaming with fire, shook his fist in his master's face. "No it is not the fatigue, you villain! It is you who have killed her, with your jezebels and harlots, you scoundrel!"

"Send the women here, James, for God's sake!" cried Mr. Vane, not even noticing the insult he had received from a servant. He stamped furiously, and cried for help. The whole household was round her in a moment. They carried her to bed.

The remorse-stricken man, his own knees trembling under him, flew, in an agony of fear and self-reproach, for a doctor!

A doctor?

CHAPTER XIII.

During the garden scene, Mr. Vane had begged Mrs. Woffington to let him accompany her. She peremptorily refused, and said in the same breath she was going to Triplet, in Hercules Buildings, to have her portrait finished.

Had Mr. Vane understood the sex, he would not have interpreted her refusal to the letter; when there was a postscript, the meaning of which was so little enigmatical.

Some three hours after the scene we have described, Mrs. Woffington sat in Triplet's apartment; and Triplet, palette in hand, painted away upon her portrait.

Mrs. Woffington was in that languid state which comes to women after their hearts have received a blow. She felt as if life was ended, and but the dregs of existence remained; but at times a flood of bitterness rolled over her, and she resigned all hope of perfect happiness in this world — all hope of loving and respecting the same creature; and at these moments she had but one idea — to use her own power, and bind her lover to her by chains never to be broken; and to close her eyes, and glide down the precipice of the future.

"I think you are master of this art," said she, very languidly, to Triplet, "you paint so rapidly."

"Yes, madam," said Triplet, gloomily; and painted on. "Confound this shadow!" added he; and painted on.

His soul, too, was clouded. Mrs. Woffington, yawning in his face, had told him she had invited all Mr. Vane's company to come and praise his work; and ever since that he had been *morne et silencieux.*

"You are fortunate," continued Mrs. Woffington, not caring what she said; "it is so difficult to make execution keep pace with conception."

"Yes, ma'am;" and he painted on.

"You are satisfied with it?"

"Any thing but, ma'am;" and he painted on.

"Cheerful soul! — then I presume it is like."

"Not a bit, ma'am;" and he painted on.

Mrs. Woffington stretched.

"You can't yawn, ma'am — you can't yawn."

"O yes, I can. You are such good company;" and she stretched again.

"I was just about to catch the turn of the lip," remonstrated Triplet.

"Well, catch it — it won't run away."

"I'll try, ma'am. A pleasant half hour it will be for me, when they all come here like cits at a shilling ordinary — each for his cut."

"At a sensitive goose!"

"That is as may be, madam. Those critics flay us alive!"

"You should not hold so many doors open to censure."

"No, ma'am. Head a little more that way. I suppose you *can't* sit quiet, ma'am? — then never mind!" (This resignation was intended as a stinging reproach.) "Mr. Cibber, with his sneering snuffbox! Mr. Quin, with his humorous bludgeon! Mrs. Clive, with her tongue! Mr. Snarl, with his abuse! And Mr. Soaper, with his praise! — arsenic in treacle I call it! But there, I deserve it all! For look on this picture, and on this!"

"Meaning, I am painted as well as my picture!"

"O no, no, no! But to turn from your face, madam — on which the lightning of expression plays continually — to this stony, detestable, dead daub! — I could — And I will, too! Imposture! dead caricature of life and beauty, take that!" and he dashed his palette knife through the canvas. "Libellous lie against nature and Mrs. Woffington, take that!" and he stabbed the canvas again; then, with sudden humility, "I beg your pardon, ma'am," said he, "for this apparent outrage, which I trust you will set down to the excitement attendant upon failure. The fact is, I am an incapable ass, and no painter! Others have often hinted as much; but I never observed it myself till now!"

"Right through my pet dimple!" said Mrs. Woffington, with perfect *nonchalance*. "Well, now I suppose I may yawn, or do what I like?"

"You may, madam," said Triplet, gravely. "I have forfeited what little control I had over you, madam."

So they sat opposite each other, in mournful silence. At length, the actress suddenly rose. She struggled fiercely against her depression, and vowed that melancholy should not benumb her spirits and her power.

"He ought to have been here by this time," said she to herself. "Well, I will not mope for him: I must do something. Triplet," said she.

"Madam."

"Nothing."

"No, madam."

She sat gently down again, and leaned her head on her hand, and thought. She was beautiful as she thought! — her body seemed bristling with mind! At last, her thoughtful gravity was illumined by a smile: she had thought out something *excogitaverat.*

"Triplet, the picture is quite ruined!"

"Yes, madam, and a coach load of criticism coming!"

"Triplet, we actors and actresses have often bright ideas."

"Yes, ma'am."

"When we take other people's!"

"He! he!" went Triplet. "Those are our best, madam!"

"Well, sir, I have got a bright idea."

"You don't say so, ma'am!"

"Don't be a brute, dear!" said the lady, gravely.

Triplet stared!

"When I was in France, taking lessons of Dumesnil, one of the actors of the Théâtre Français had his portrait painted, by a rising artist. The others were to come and see it. They determined, beforehand, to mortify the painter and the sitter, by abusing the work in good set terms. But somehow this got wind, and the patients resolved to be the physicians. They put their heads together, and contrived that the living face should be in the canvas, surrounded by the accessories: these, of course, were painted. Enter the actors, who played their little pre-arranged farce; and when they had each given the picture a slap, the picture rose and laughed in their faces, and discomfited them! By the by, the painter did not stop there: he was not content with a short laugh; he laughed at them five hundred years!"

"Good gracious, Mrs. Woffington."

"He painted a picture of the whole thing; and as his work is immortal, ours an April snowflake, he has got tremendously the better of those rash little satirists. Well, Trip, what is sauce for the gander is sauce for the goose; so give me the sharpest knife in the house."

Triplet gave her a knife, and looked confused, while she cut away the face of the picture, and by dint of scraping, cutting, and measuring, got her face two parts through the canvas. She then made him take his brush and paint all round her face, so that the transition might not be too abrupt. Several yards of green baize were also produced. This was to be disposed behind the easel, so as to conceal her.

Triplet painted here, and touched and re-touched there. Whilst thus occupied, he said, in his calm, resigned way, "It won't do, madam. I suppose you know that."

"I know nothing," was the reply. "Life is a guess. I don't think we could deceive Roxalana and Lucy this way, because their eyes are without colored spectacles; but when people have once begun to see by prejudices and judge by jargon, what can't be done with them? Who knows? Do you? I don't; so let us try."

"I beg your pardon, madam; my brush touched your face."

"No offence, sir; I am used to that. And I beg, if you can't tone the rest of the picture up to me, that you will instantly tone me down to the rest. Let us be in tune, whatever it costs, sir."

"I will avail myself of the privilege, madam, but sparingly. Failure, which is certain, madam, will cover us with disgrace."

"Nothing is certain in this life, sir, except that you are a goose. It succeeded in France; and England can match all Europe for fools. Besides, it will be well done. They say Davy Garrick can turn his eyes into bottled gooseberries. Well, Peg Woffington will turn hers into black currants. Haven't you done? I wonder they have not come. Make haste!"

"They will know by its beauty I never did it."

"That is a sensible remark, Trip. But I think they will rather argue backwards; that as you did it, it cannot be beautiful, and so cannot be me. Your reputation will be our shield."

"Well, madam, now you mention it, they are like enough to take that ground. They despise all I do; if they did not ——"

"You would despise them."

At this moment the pair were startled by the sound of a coach. Triplet turned as pale as ashes. Mrs. Woffington had her misgivings;

but not choosing to increase the difficulty, she would not let Triplet, whose self-possession she doubted, see any sign of emotion in her.

"Lock the door," said she, firmly, "and don't be silly. Now hold up my green baize petticoat, and let me be in a half light. Now put that table and those chairs before me, so that they can't come right up to me; and, Triplet, don't let them come within six yards, if you can help it. Say it is unfinished, and so must be seen from a focus."

"A focus! I don't know what you mean."

"No more do I; no more will they, perhaps; and if they don't, they will swallow it directly. Unlock the door: are they coming?"

"They are only at the first stair."

"Mr. Triplet, your face is a book, where one may read strange matters. For Heaven's sake compose yourself; let all the risk lie in one countenance. Look at me, sir. Make your face like the book of Daniel in a Jew's back parlor. Volto Sciolto is your cue."

"Madam, madam, how your tongue goes! I hear them on the stairs: pray don't speak!"

"Do you know what we are going to do?"

continued the tormenting Peggy. "We are going to weigh gooses feathers! to criticize criticism, Trip ——"

"Hush! hush!"

A grampus was heard outside the door, and Triplet opened it. There was Quin leading the band.

"Have a care, sir," cried Triplet; "there is a hiatus the third step from the door."

"A *gradus ad Parnassum* a wanting," said Mr. Cibber.

Triplet's heart sank. The hole had been there six months, and he had found nothing witty to say about it, and at first sight Mr. Cibber had done its business. And on such men he and his portrait were to attempt a preposterous delusion. Then there was Snarl, who wrote critiques on painting, and guided the national taste. The unlucky exhibitor was in a cold sweat. He led the way like a thief going to the gallows.

"The picture, being unfinished, gentlemen," said he, "must, if you would do me justice, be seen from a — a focus; must be judged from here, I mean."

"Where, sir?" said Mr. Cibber.

"About here, sir, if you please," said pooı Triplet, faintly.

"It looks like a finished picture from here," said Mrs. Clive.

"Yes, madam," groaned Triplet.

They all took up a position, and Triplet timid ly raised his eyes along with the rest: he was a little surprised. The actress had flattened her face! She had done all that could be done, and more than he had conceived possible, in the way of extracting life and the atmosphere of expression from her countenance. She was "dead still!"

There was a pause.

Triplet fluttered. At last some of them spoke as follows: —

SOAPER. — Ah!

QUIN. — Ho!

CLIVE. — Eh!

CIBBER. — Humph!

These interjections are small on paper, but as the good creatures uttered them they were eloquent; there was a cheerful variety of dispraise skilfully thrown into each of them.

"Well," continued Soaper, with his everlasting smile.

Then the fun began.

"May I be permitted to ask whose portrait this is?" said Mr. Cibber, slyly.

"I distinctly told you it was to be Peg Woffington's," said Mrs. Clive. "I think you might take my word."

"Do you act as truly as you paint?" said Quin.

"Your fame runs no risk from me, sir!" replied Triplet.

"It is not like Peggy's beauty! Eh?" rejoined Quin.

"I can't agree with you," cried Kitty Clive. "I think it a very pretty face; and not at all like Peg Woffington's."

"Compare paint with paint," said Quin. "Are you sure you ever saw down to Peggy's real face?"

Triplet had seen with alarm, that Mr. Snarl spoke not: many satirical expressions crossed his face, but he said nothing. Triplet gathered from this that he had at once detected the trick. "Ah!" thought Triplet, "he means to quiz them, as well as expose me. He is hanging back; and, in point of fact, a mighty satirist like

Snarl would naturally choose to quiz six peopl rather than two."

"Now, I call it beautiful!" said the traitor Soaper. "So calm and reposeful; no particular expression."

"None whatever," said Snarl.

"Gentlemen," said Triplet, "does it never occur to you, that the fine arts are tender violets, and cannot blow when the north winds ——"

"Blow!" inserted Quin.

"Are so cursed cutting?" continued Triplet.

"My good sir, I am never cutting!" smirked Soaper. "My dear Snarl," whined he, "give us the benefit of your practised judgment. Do justice to this ad-mirable work of art," drawled the traitor.

"I will!" said Mr. Snarl; and placed himself before the picture.

"What on earth will he say?" thought Triplet. "I can see by his face he has found us out."

Mr. Snarl delivered a short critique. Mr. Snarl's intelligence was not confined to his phrases; all critics use intelligent phrases and philosophical truths. But this gentleman's man-ıer was very intelligent; it was pleasant, quiet, ıssured, and very convincing. Had the reader ɔr I been there, he would have carried us with him, as he did his hearers; and as his successors carry the public with them now.

"Your brush is by no means destitute of talent, Mr. Triplet," said Mr. Snarl. "But you are somewhat deficient, at present, in the great principles of your art; the first of which is a loyal adherence to truth. Beauty itself is but one of the forms of truth, and nature is our finite exponent of infinite truth."

His auditors gave him a marked attention. They could not but acknowledge that men who go to the bottom of things like this should be the best instructors.

"Now, in nature, a woman's face at this distance — ay, even at this short distance — melts into the air. There is none of that sharpness; but, on the contrary, a softness of outline." He made a lorgnette of his two hands; the others did so too, and found they saw much better — O, ever so much better! "Whereas, yours," resumed Snarl, "is hard; and, forgive me, rather tea-board like. Then your *chiaro scuro*, my good sir, is very defective; for instance, in nature, the nose intercepting the light on one side the face throws, of necessity, a shadow under the eye. Caravaggio, Venetians generally, and the Bolognese masters, do particular justice to this. No such shade appears in this portrait."

"'Tis so, stop my vitals!" observed Colley Cibber. And they all looked, and having looked, wagged their heads in assent — as the fat, white lords at Christie's waggle fifty pounds more out for a copy of Rembrandt, a brown levitical Dutchman, visible in the pitch dark by some sleight of sun Newton had not wit to discover.

Soaper dissented from the mass.

"But, my dear Snarl, if there are no shades, there are lights, loads of lights."

"There are," replied Snarl; "only they are impossible, that is all. You have, however," concluded he, with a manner slightly supercilious, "succeeded in the mechanical parts: the hair and the dress are well, Mr. Triplet; but *your* Woffington is not a woman, nor nature."

They all nodded and waggled assent; but this sagacious motion was arrested as by an earthquake.

The picture rang out, in the voice of a clarion, an answer that outlived the speaker, "She's a woman! for she has taken four men in! She's nature! for a fluent dunce doesn't know her when he sees her!"

Imagine the tableau! It was charming! Such opening of eyes and mouths! Cibber fell by second nature into an attitude of the old comedy. And all were rooted where they stood, with surprise and incipient mortification, except Quin, who slapped his knee, and took the trick at its value.

Peg Woffington slipped out of the green baize, and coming round from the back of the late picture, stood in person before them; while they looked alternately at her and at the hole in the canvas. She then came at each of them in turn, *more dramatico.*

"A pretty face, and not like Woffington. I owe you two, Kate Clive."

"Who ever saw Peggy's real face? Look at it now if you can without blushing, Mr. Quin."

Quin, a good-humored fellow, took the wisest view of his predicament, and burst into a hearty laugh.

"For all this," said Mr. Snarl, peevishly, "I maintain, upon the unalterable principles of art——" At this they all burst into a roar, not sorry to shift the ridicule. "Goths!" cried Snarl, fiercely. "Good morning, ladies and gentlemen," cried Mr. Snarl, *avec intention*, "I have a criticism to write of last night's performance." The laugh died away to a quaver. "I shall sit on your pictures one day, Mr. Brush."

"Don't sit on them with your head downwards, or you'll addle them," said Mr. Brush, fiercely. This was the first time Triplet had ever answered a foe. Mrs. Woffington gave him an eloquent glance of encouragement. He nodded his head in infantine exultation at what he had done.

"Come, Soaper," said Mr. Snarl.

Mr. Soaper lingered one moment to say, "You shall always have my good word, Mr. Triplet."

"I will try—and not deserve it, Mr. Soaper," was the prompt reply.

"Serve 'em right," said Mr. Cibber, as soon as the door had closed upon them, "for a couple of serpents, or rather one boa constrictor. Soaper slavers, for Snarl to crush. But we were all a little too hard on Triplet here; and if he will accept my apology——"

"Why, sir," said Triplet, half trembling, but iven on by looks from Mrs. Woffington, "'Cibber's Apology' is found to be a trifle weariome."

"Confound his impertinence!" cried the asounded laureate. "Come along, Jemmy."

"O sir!" said Quin, good humoredly, "we must give a joke and take a joke. And when he paints my portrait — which he shall do ——"

"The bear from Hockley Hole shall sit for the head!"

"Curse his impudence!" roared Quin. "I'm at your service, Mr. Cibber," added he, in huge dudgeon.

Away went the two old boys.

"Mighty well!" said waspish Mrs. Clive. "I did intend you should have painted Mrs. Clive. But after this impertinence ——"

"You will continue to do it yourself, ma'am."

This was Triplet's hour of triumph. His exultation was undignified, and such as is said to precede a fall. He inquired gravely of Mrs. Woffington, whether he had or had not shown a spirit? Whether he had or had not fired into each a parting shot, as they sheered off? To repair which, it might be advisable for them put into friendly ports.

" Tremendous ! " was the reply. " And whe Snarl and Soaper sit on your next play, the won't forget the lesson you have given them."

" I'll be sworn they won't ! " chuckled Triplet But reconsidering her words, he looked blank and muttered, " Then, perhaps, it would have been more prudent to let them alone ! "

" Incalculably more prudent ! " was the reply.

" Then why did you set me on, madam ? " said Triplet, reproachfully.

" Because I wanted amusement, and my head ached," was the cool answer, somewhat languidly given.

" I defy the coxcombs ! " cried Triplet, with reviving spirit. " But real criticism I respect, honor, and bow to. Such as yours, madam ; or such as that sweet lady's at Mr. Vane's would have been ; or, in fact, any body's who appreciates me. O madam, I wanted to ask you, was it not strange your not being at Mr. Vane's, after all, to-day ? "

" I was at Mr. Vane's, Triplet."

" You were ? Why, I came with my verses,

ıd she said you were not there! I will go fetch ıe verses."

"No, no! Who said I was not there?"

"Did I not tell you? The charming young ıdy who helped me with her own hand to every hing on the table. What wine that gentleman ›ossesses!"

"Was it a young lady, Triplet?"

"Not more than two and twenty, I should say."

"In a travelling dress?"

"I could not see her dress, madam, for her beauty — brown hair, blue eyes, charming in conversation ——"

"Ah! What did she tell you?"

"She told me, madam — Ahem!"

"Well, what did you tell her? And what did she answer?"

"I told her that I came with verses for you, ordered by Mr. Vane. That he admired you. I descanted, madam, on your virtues, which had made him your slave."

"Go on," said Mrs. Woffington, encouraging him with a deceitful smile. "Tell me all you told her."

"That you were sitting to me for your po: trait, the destination of which was not doubtfu That I lived at 10, Hercules Buildings."

"You told that lady all this?"

"I give you my honor. She was so kind I opened my heart to her. But tell me now madam," said Triplet, joyously dancing rounc the Woffington volcano, "do you know this charming lady?"

"Yes."

"I congratulate you, madam. An acquaintance worthy even of you; and there are not many such. Who is she, madam?" continued Triplet, lively with curiosity.

"Mrs. Vane," was the quiet, grim answer.

"Mrs. Vane? His mother? No — am I mad? His sister! O, I see, his ——"

"His wife!"

"His wife! Why, then Mr. Vane's married?"

"Yes."

"O, look there! — O, look here now! Well, but, good Heavens! she wasn't to know you were there, perhaps?"

"No."

"But then, I let the cat out of the bag?"

"Yes."

"But, good gracious! there will be some se-ous mischief?"

"No doubt of it."

"And it is all my fault?"

"Yes."

"I've played the deuse with their married hap-piness."

"Probably."

"And ten to one if you are not incensed against me too?"

Mrs. Woffington replied by looking him in the face, and turning her back upon him. She walked hastily to the window, threw it open, and looked out of it; leaving poor Triplet to very unpleasant reflections. She was so angry with him, she dared not trust herself to speak.

"Just my luck," thought he. "I had a patron and a benefactress — I have betrayed them both." Suddenly an idea struck him: "Madam," said he, timorously, "see what these fine gentlemen are! What business had he, with a wife at home, to come and fall in love with you? I do it forever in my plays — I am obliged —

they would be so dull else; but in *real* life to it is abominable."

"You forget, sir," replied Mrs. Woffingto without moving, "that I am an actress — a pla thing for the impertinence of puppies, and tl treachery of hypocrites. Fool! to think thei was an honest man in the world, and that he ha shone on me."

With these words she turned, and Triplet wa shocked to see the change in her face. She wa pale, and her black, lowering brows were gloomy and terrible. She walked like a tigress to anc fro, and Triplet dared not speak to her: indeed, she seemed but half conscious of his presence. He went for nobody with her. How little we know the people we eat, and go to church, and flirt with! Triplet had imagined this creature an incarnation of gayety, a sportive being, the daughter of smiles, the bride of mirth; needed but a look at her now to see that her heart was a volcano, her bosom a boiling gulf of fiery lava. She walked like some wild creature; she flung her hands up to heaven with a passionate despair, before which the feeble spirit of her companion shrank and cowered; and with quivering lips and

.azing eyes, she burst into a torrent of passion-:e bitterness :—

"But who is Margaret Woffington," she cried, that she should pretend to honest love, or feel nsulted by the proffer of a stolen regard? And vhat have we to do with homes, or hearts, or iresides? Have we not the playhouse, its paste liamonds, its paste feelings, and the loud applause of fops and sots — hearts? — beneath loads of tinsel and paint? Nonsense! The love that can go with souls to heaven — such love for us? Nonsense! These men applaud us, cajole us, swear to us, flatter us; and yet, forsooth, we would have them respect us too."

"My dear benefactress," said Triplet, "they are not worthy of you."

"I thought this man was not all dross; from the first I never felt his passion an insult. O Triplet! I could have loved this man — really loved him! and I longed so to be good. O God! O God!"

"Thank Heaven, you don't love him!" cried Triplet, hastily. "Thank Heaven for that!"

"Love him? Love a man who comes to me with a silly second-hand affection from his insipid baby face, and offers me half, or two thirds, or third of his worthless heart? I hate him! — an her! — and all the world!"

"That is what I call a very proper feeling,' said poor Triplet, with a weak attempt to sooth her. "Then break with him at once, and al will be well."

"Break with him? Are you mad? No! Since he plays with the tools of my trade, I shall fool him worse than he has me. I will feed his passion full, tempt him, torture him, play with him, as the angler plays a fish upon his hook. And when his very life depends on me, then by degrees he shall see me cool, and cool, and freeze into bitter aversion. Then he shall rue the hour he fought with the devil against my soul, and played false with a brain and heart like mine!"

"But his poor wife? You will have pity on her?"

"His wife! Are wives' hearts the only hearts that throb, and burn, and break? His wife must defend herself. It is not from me that mercy can come to her, nor from her to me. I loathe her, and I shall not forget that you took her part. Only if you are her friend, take my advice, don't you assist her. I shall defeat her without that. Let her fight *her* battle, and ***I*** mine."

"Ah, madam! she cannot fight; she is a dove."

"You are a fool! What do you know about women? You were with her five minutes, and she turned you inside out. My life on it, whilst I have been fooling my time here, she is in the field, with all the arts of our sex, simplicity at the head of them."

Triplet was making a futile endeavor to convert her to his view of her rival, when a knock suddenly came to his door. A slovenly girl, one of his own neighbors, brought him a bit of paper, with a line written in pencil.

"'Tis from a lady, who waits below," said the girl.

Mrs. Woffington went again to the window, and there she saw getting out of a coach, and attended by James Burdock, Mabel Vane, who had sent up her name on the back of an old letter.

"What shall I do?" said Triplet, as soon as he recovered the first stunning effects of this *contre-temps*. To his astonishment, Mrs. Woffington bade the girl show the lady up stairs. The girl went down on this errand.

"But *you* are here," remonstrated Triplet "O! to be sure, you can go into the other room There is plenty of time to avoid her," said Triplet, in a very natural tremor. "This way, madam!"

Mrs. Woffington stood in the middle of the room like a statue.

"What does she come here for?" said she, sternly. "You have not told me all."

"I don't know," cried poor Triplet, in dismay; "and I think the devil brings her here to confound me. For Heaven's sake, retire! What will become of us all? There will be murder, I know there will!"

To his horror, Mrs. Woffington would not move. "You are on her side," said she, slowly, with a concentration of spite and suspicion. She looked frightful at this moment. "All the better for me," added she, with a world of female malignity.

Triplet could not make head against this blow; he gasped, and pointed piteously to the inner door. "No; I will know two things: the course she means to take, and the terms you two are upon."

By this time, Mrs. Vane's light foot was heard on the stair, and Triplet sank into a chair. "They will tear one another to pieces," said he.

A tap came to the door.

He looked fearfully round for the woman whom jealousy had so speedily turned from an angel to a fiend, and saw with dismay that she had actually had the hardihood to slip round and enter the picture again. She had not quite arranged herself when her rival knocked.

Triplet dragged himself to the door. Before he opened it, he looked fearfully over his shoulder, and received a glance of cool, bitter, deadly hostility, that boded ill both for him and his visitor. Triplet's apprehensions were not unreasonable. His benefactress and this sweet lady were rivals!

Jealousy is a dreadful passion; it makes us tigers. The jealous always thirst for blood. At any moment, when reason is a little weaker than usual, they are ready to kill the thing they hate, or the thing they love.

Any open collision between these ladies would scatter ill consequences all round. Under such circumstances, we are pretty sure to say or do something wicked, silly, or unreasonable. Bu what tortured Triplet more than any thing, wa. his own particular notion that fate doomed hin to witness a formal encounter between these twc women; and, of course, an encounter of such a nature as we in our day illustrate by "Kilkenny cats."

To be sure Mrs. Vane had appeared a dove, but doves can peck on certain occasions, and no doubt she had a spirit at bottom. Her coming to him proved it. And had not the other been a dove all the morning and afternoon? Yet jealousy had turned her to a fiend before his eyes Then if (which was not probable) no collision took place, what a situation was his? Mrs. Woffington (his buckler from starvation) suspected him, and would distort every word that came from Mrs. Vane's lips.

Triplet's situation was, in fact, that of Æneas in the storm.

"Olim et hac meminisse juvabit ——"
"But while present, such things don't please any one a bit."

It was a sort of situation we can laugh at, and

ee the fun of it six months after, if not ship-vrecked on it at the time.

With a ghastly smile the poor quaking hypo-:rite welcomed Mrs. Vane, and professed a world of innocent delight that she had so honored his humble roof.

She interrupted his compliments, and begged him to see whether she was followed by a gen tleman in a cloak.

Triplet looked out of the window.

"Sir Charles Pomander," gasped he.

Sir Charles was at the very door. If, however, he had intended to mount the stairs, he changed his mind; for he suddenly went off round the corner with a business-like air, real or fictitious.

"He is gone, madam," said Triplet.

Mrs. Vane, the better to escape detection or observation, wore a thick mantle and a hood, that concealed her features. Of these Triplet debarrassed her.

"Sit down, madam," and he hastily drew a chair, so that her back was to the picture.

She was pale, and trembled a little. She hid her face in her hands a moment; then recovering her courage, "she begged Mr. Triplet to pardon her for coming to him. He had inspired he with confidence," she said; "he had offered he. his services, and so she had come to him; for sh(had no other friend to aid her in her sore dis· tress." She might have added, that with thε tact of her sex she had read Triplet to the bottom, and came to him as she would to a benevolent muscular old woman.

Triplet's natural impulse was to repeat most warmly his offers of service. He did so; and then, conscious of the picture, had a misgiving.

"Dear Mr. Triplet," began Mrs. Vane, "you know this person, Mrs. Woffington?"

"Yes, madam," replied Triplet, lowering his eyes, "I am honored by her acquaintance."

"You will take me to the theatre where she acts?"

"Yes, madam; to the boxes, I presume?"

"No; O, no! How could I bear that? To the place where the actors and actresses are."

Triplet demurred. This would be courting that very collision the dread of which even now oppressed him.

At the first faint sign of resistance she began

to supplicate him, as if he was some great stern tyrant.

"O, you must not, you cannot refuse me. You do not know what I risk to obtain this. I have risen from my bed to come to you. I have a fire here!" She pressed her hand to her brow. "O, take me to her!"

"Madam, I will do any thing for you. But be advised; trust to my knowledge of human nature. What you require is madness. Gracious Heavens! you two are rivals; and when rivals meet there's murder or deadly mischief."

"Ah! if you knew my sorrow, you would not thwart me. O, Mr. Triplet! little did I think you were as cruel as the rest." So then this cruel monster whimpered out, that he should do any folly she insisted upon. "Good, kind Mr. Triplet!" said Mrs. Vane. "Let me look in your face! Yes; I see you are honest and true. I will tell you all." Then she poured in his ear her simple tale, unadorned and touching as Judah's speech to Joseph. She told him how she loved her husband; how he had loved her; how happy they were for the first six months; how her heart sank when he left her; how he had promised she should join him, and on that hope she lived. "But for two months he had ceased to speak of this, and I grew heart sick waiting for the summons that never came. At last I felt I should die if I did not see him; so I plucked up courage, and wrote that I must come to him. He did not forbid me, so I left our country home. O, sir, I cannot make you know how my heart burned to be by his side! I counted the hours of the journey; I counted the miles. At last I reached his house; I found a gay company there. I was a little sorry; but I said, 'His friends shall be welcome, right welcome. He has asked them to welcome his wife.'"

"Poor thing!" muttered Triplet.

"O, Mr. Triplet! they were there to do honor to ——, and the wife was neither expected nor desired. There lay my letters, with their seals unbroken. I know all *his* letters by heart, Mr. Triplet. The seals unbroken — unbroken! Mr. Triplet."

"It is abominable!" cried Triplet, fiercely.

"And she who sat in my seat — in his house and in his heart — was this lady, the actress you so praised to me!"

"That lady, ma'am," said Triplet, "has been deceived as well as you."

"I am convinced of it," said Mabel.

"And it is my painful duty to tell you, madam, that with all her talents and sweetness, she has a fiery temper; yes, a very fiery temper," continued Triplet, stoutly, though with an uneasy glance in a certain direction; "and I have reason to believe she is angry, and thinks more of her own ill usage than yours. Don't you go near her. Trust to my knowledge of the sex, madam; I am a dramatic writer. Did you ever read the 'Rival Queens'?"

"No."

"I thought not. Well, madam, one stabs the other, and the one that is stabbed says things to the other that are more biting than steel. The prudent course for you is to keep apart, and be always cheerful, and welcome him with a smile — and — have you read 'The Way to keep him'?"

"No, Mr. Triplet," said Mabel, firmly; "I cannot feign. Were I to attempt talent and deceit, I should be weaker than I am now. Honesty and right are all my strength. I will cry to

her for justice and mercy. And if I cry in vai
I shall die, Mr. Triplet, that is all."

"Don't cry, dear lady," said Triplet, in a bro
ken voice.

"It is impossible!" cried she, suddenly. "
am not learned, but I can read faces. I alway
could, and so could my aunt Deborah before me
I read you right, Mr. Triplet, and I have read
her too. Did not my heart warm to her amongst
them all? There *is* a heart at the bottom of all her acting, and that heart is good and noble."

"She is, madam! she is! and charitable too. I know a family she saved from starvation and despair. O, yes; she has a heart — to feel for the *poor*, at all events."

"And am I not the poorest of the poor?" cried Mrs. Vane. "I have no father nor mother, Mr. Triplet; my husband is all I have in the world — all I *had*, I mean."

Triplet, deeply affected himself, stole a look at Mrs. Woffington. She was pale; but her face was composed into a sort of dogged obstinacy. He was disgusted with her. "Madam," said he, sternly, there is a wild beast more cruel and savıge than wolves and bears; it is called 'a rival,' ınd don't you get in its way."

At this moment, in spite of Triplet's precaution, Mrs. Vane, casting her eye accidentally round, caught sight of the picture, and instantly started up, crying, "She is there!" Triplet was thunderstruck. "What a likeness!" cried she, and moved towards the supposed picture.

"Don't go to it!" cried Triplet, aghast; "the color is wet."

She stopped; but her eye, and her very soul, dwelt upon the supposed picture; and Triplet stood quaking. "How like! It seems to breathe. You are a good painter, sir. A glass is not truer."

Triplet, hardly knowing what he said, muttered something about "critics, and lights and shades."

"Then they are blind!" cried Mabel, never for a moment removing her eye from the object. "Tell me not of lights and shades. The pictures I see have a look of paint; but yours looks like life. O that she were here, as this *wonderful* image of hers is. I would speak to her. I am not wise or learned; but orators never pleaded as

I would plead to her for my Ernest's heart.' Still her eye glanced upon the picture; and, I suppose, her heart realized an actual presence, though her judgment did not; for by some irresistible impulse she sank slowly down, and stretched her clasped hands towards it, while sobs and words seemed to break direct from her bursting heart. "O, yes! you are beautiful, you are gifted, and the eyes of thousands wait upon your every word and look. What wonder that he, ardent, refined, and genial, should lay his heart at your feet? And I have nothing but my love to make him love me. I cannot take him from you. O, be generous to the weak! O, give him back to me! What is one heart more to you? You are so rich, and I am so poor, that without his love I have nothing, and can do nothing but sit me down and cry till my heart breaks. Give him back to me, beautiful, terrible woman! for, with all your gifts, you cannot love him as his poor Mabel does; and I will love you longer, perhaps, than men can love. I will kiss your feet, and Heaven above will bless you; and I will bless you and pray for you to my dying day. Ah! it is alive! I am frightened! I am frightned!" She ran to Triplet, and seized his arm. 'No!" cried she, quivering close to him; "I'm not frightened, for it was for me she—— O Mrs. Woffington!" and hiding her face on Mr. Triplet's shoulder, she blushed, and wept, and trembled.

What was it had betrayed Mrs. Woffington? *A tear!*

During the whole of this interview (which had taken a turn so unlooked for by the listener) she might have said, with Beatrice, "What fire is in mine ears!" and what self-reproach and chill misgiving in her heart, too! She had passed through a hundred emotions, as the young, innocent wife told her sad and simple story. But anxious now above all things to escape without being recognized,—for she had long repented having listened at all, or placed herself in her present position,—she fiercely mastered her countenance; but though she ruled her features, she could not rule her heart. And when the young wife, instead of inveighing against her, came to her as a supplicant, with faith in her goodness, and sobbed to her for pity, a big tear rolled down her cheek, and proved her something more tha: a picture or an actress.

Mrs. Vane, as we have related, screamed, an ran to Triplet.

Mrs. Woffington came instantly from her frame and stood before them in a despairing attitude with one hand upon her brow. For a single moment her impulse was to fly from the apartment, so ashamed was she of having listened, and of meeting her rival in this way; but she conquered this feeling, and as soon as she saw Mrs. Vane too had recovered some composure, she said to Triplet, in a low but firm voice,—

"Leave us, sir. No living creature must hear what I say to this lady!"

Triplet remonstrated, but Mrs. Vane said, faintly,—

"O, yes, good Mr. Triplet, I would rather you left me."

Triplet, full of misgivings, was obliged to retire.

"Be composed, ladies," said he, piteously. "Neither of you could help it;" and so he entered his inner room, where he sat and listened ervously, for he could not shake off all appre-ension of a personal encounter.

In the room he had left, there was a long, un-easy silence. Both ladies were greatly embar-rassed. It was the actress who spoke first. All trace of emotion, except a certain pallor, was driv-en from her face. She spoke with very marked courtesy, but in tones that seemed to freeze as they dropped one by one from her mouth.

"I trust, madam, you will do me the justice to believe I did not know Mr. Vane was married?"

"I am sure of it!" said Mabel, warmly. "I feel you are as good as you are gifted."

"Mrs. Vane, I am not!" said the other, almost sternly. "You are deceived!"

"Then Heaven have mercy on me! No! I am not deceived; you pitied me. You speak coldly now; but I know your face and your heart — you pity me!"

"I do respect, admire, and pity you," said Mrs. Woffington, sadly; "and I could consent never more to communicate with your — with Mr. Vane."

"Ah!" cried Mabel, "Heaven will bless you! But will you give me back his heart?"

"How can I do that?" said Mrs. Woffington uneasily; she had not bargained for this.

"The magnet can repel as well as attract. Can you not break your own spell? What will his presence be to me, if his heart remain behind?"

"You ask much of me."

"Alas! I do."

"But I could do even this." She paused for breath. "And perhaps if you, who have not only touched my heart, but won my respect, were to say to me, 'Do so,' I should do it." Again she paused, and spoke with difficulty; for the bitter struggle took away her breath. "Mr. Vane thinks better of me than I deserve. I have — only — to make him believe me — worthless — worse than I am — and he will drop me like an adder — and love you better, far better — for having known — admired — and despised Margaret Woffington."

"O!" cried Mabel, "I shall bless you every hour of my life." Her countenance brightened into rapture at the picture, and Mrs. Woffington's darkened with bitterness as she watched her.

But Mabel reflected. "Rob you of your good

ıme?" said this pure creature. "Ah, Mabel 'ane, you think but of yourself!"

"I thank you, madam," said Mrs. Woffington, little touched by this unexpected trait; "but ome one must suffer here, and——"

Mabel Vane interrupted her. "This would ɔe cruel and base," said she, firmly. "No woman's forehead shall be soiled by me. O madam! beauty is admired, talent is adored; but virtue is a woman's crown. With it the poor are rich; without it the rich are poor. It walks through life upright, and never hides its head for high or low."

Her face was as the face of an angel now; and the actress, conquered by her beauty and her goodness, actually bowed her head, and gently kissed the hand of the country wife whom she had quizzed a few hours ago.

Frailty paid this homage to virtue!

Mabel Vane hardly noticed it; her eye was lifted to heaven, and her heart was gone there for help in a sore struggle.

"This would be to assassinate you; no less. And so, madam," she sighed, "with God's help, I do refuse your offer; choosing rather, if needs be, to live desolate, but innocent — many a be ter than I have lived so — ay! if God wills it, die, with my hopes and my heart crushed, bı my hands unstained; for so my humble life hε passed."

How beautiful, great, and pure goodness is It paints heaven on the face that has it; i wakens the sleeping souls that meet it.

At the bottom of Margaret Woffington's heart lay a soul, unknown to the world, scarce known to herself — a heavenly harp, on which ill airs of passion had been played; but still it was there, in tune with all that is true, pure, really great and good. And now the flush that a great heart sends to the brow, to herald great actions, came to her cheek and brow.

"Humble!" she cried. "Such as you are the diamonds of our race. You angel of truth and goodness, you have conquered!"

"O, yes, yes! Thank God, yes!"

"What a fiend I must be could I injure you! The poor heart we have both overrated shall be yours again, and yours forever. In my hands it is painted glass; in the lustre of a love like yours it may become a priceless jewel." She rned her head away, and pondered a moment, ien suddenly offered to Mrs. Vane her hand ith nobleness and majesty: "Can you trust ie?" The actress too was divinely beautiful iow, for her good angel shone through her.

"I could trust you with my life!" was the eply.

"Ah! if I might call you friend, dear lady, what would I not do — suffer — resign — to be worthy that title!"

"No, not friend!" cried the warm, innocent Mabel; "sister! I will call you sister. I have no sister."

"Sister!" said Mrs. Woffington. "O, do not mock me! Alas! you do not know what you say. That sacred name to me, from lips so pure as yours — Mrs. Vane," said she, timidly, "would you think me presumptuous if I begged you to — to let me kiss you?"

The words were scarce spoken before Mrs. Vane's arms were wreathed round her neck, and that innocent cheek laid sweetly to hers.

Mrs. Woffington strained her to her bosom, and two great hearts, whose grandeur the world, worshipper of charlatans, never discovered, had found each other out and beat against each othe. A great heart is as quick to find another out a the world is slow.

Mrs. Woffington burst into a passion of tears and clasped Mabel tighter and tighter, in a half despairing way. Mabel mistook the cause, but she kissed her tears away.

"Dear sister," said she, "be comforted. I love you. My heart warmed to you the first moment I saw you. A woman's love and gratitude are something. Ah! you will never find me change. This is for life, look you."

"God grant it!" cried the other poor woman. "O, it is not that, it is not that; it is because I am so little worthy of this. It is a sin to deceive you. I am not good like you. You do not know me!"

"You do not know yourself if you say so!" cried Mabel; and to her hearer the words seemed to come from heaven. "I read faces," said Mabel. "I read yours at sight, and you are what I set you down; and nobody must breathe a word against you, not even yourself. Do you think I am blind? You are beautiful, you are good, you are my sister, and I love you!"

"Heaven forgive me!" thought the other. How can I resign this angel's good opinion? urely Heaven sends this blessed dew to my arched heart!" And now she burned to make ood her promise, and earn this virtuous wife's ove. She folded her once more in her arms, and hen taking her by the hand, led her tenderly nto Triplet's inner room. She made her lie lown on the bed, and placed pillows high for her like a mother, and leaned over her as she lay, and pressed her lips gently to her forehead. Her fertile brain had already digested a plan, but she had resolved that this pure and candid soul should take no lessons of deceit. "Lie there," said she, "till I open the door, and then join us. Do you know what I am going to do? I am not going to restore you your husband's heart, but to show you it never really left you. You read faces; well, I read circumstances. Matters are not as you thought," said she, with all a woman's tact. "I cannot explain, but you will see." She then gave Mrs. Triplet peremptory orders not to let her charge rise from the bed until the preconcerted signal.

Mrs. Vane was, in fact, so exhausted by all

she had gone through, that she was in no conc tion to resist. She cast a look of childlike co fidence upon her rival, and then closed her eye and tried not to tremble all over and listen like frightened hare.

It is one great characteristic of genius to do great things with little things. Paxton could see that so small a matter as a greenhouse could be dilated into a crystal palace, and with two common materials — glass and iron — he raised the palace of the genii; the brightest idea and the noblest ornament added to Europe in this century, — the koh-i-nor of the west. Livy's definition of Archimedes goes on the same ground.

Peg Woffington was a genius in her way. On entering Triplet's studio her eye fell upon three trifles — Mrs. Vane's hood and mantle, the back of an old letter, and Mr. Triplet. (It will be seen how she worked these slight materials.) On the letter were written in pencil simply these wo words, "Mabel Vane." Mrs. Woffington rote above these words two more, "Alone and nprotected." She put this into Mr. Triplet's and, and bade him take it down stairs and give t Sir Charles Pomander, whose retreat, she knew, nust have been fictitious. "You will find him ound the corner," said she, "or in some shop that looks this way." Whilst uttering these words she had put on Mrs. Vane's hood and mantle.

No answer was returned, and no Triplet went out of the door.

She turned, and there he was kneeling on both knees close under her.

"Bid me jump out of that window, madam; bid me kill those two gentlemen, and I will not rebel. You are a great lady, a talented lady; you have been insulted, and no doubt blood will flow. It ought — it is your due; but that innocent lady, do not compromise her!"

"O Mr. Triplet, you need not kneel to me. I do not wish to force you to render me a service. I have no right to dictate to you."

"O, dear!" cried Triplet, "don't talk in that way. I owe you my life, but I think of your own peace of mind, for you are not one to b happy if you injure the innocent!" He rose suc denly, and cried, "madam, promise me not t stir till I come back!"

"Where are you going?"

"To bring the husband to his wife's feet, anc so save one angel from despair, and anothei angel from a great crime."

"Well, I suppose you are wiser than me," said she. "But if you are in earnest, you had better be quick, for somehow I am rather changeable about these people."

"You can't help that, madam; it is your sex; you are an angel. May I be permitted to kiss your hand? You are all goodness and gentleness at bottom. I fly to Mr. Vane, and we will be back before you have time to repent, and give the devil the upper hand again, my dear, good, sweet lady!"

Away flew Triplet, all unconscious that he was not Mrs. Woffington's opponent, but puppet. He ran, he tore, animated by a good action, and spurred by the notion that he was in direct competition with the fiend for the possession of his benefactress.

He had no sooner turned the corner than Mrs. Woffington, looking out of the window, observed Sir Charles Pomander on the watch, as she had expected. She remained at the window with Mrs. Vane's hood on, until Sir Charles's eye in its wanderings lighted on her, and then dropping Mrs. Vane's letter from the window she hastily withdrew.

Sir Charles eagerly picked it up. His eye brightened when he read the short contents. With a self-satisfied smile he mounted the stair. He found in Triplet's house a lady, who seemed startled at her late hardihood. She sat with her back to the door, her hood drawn tightly down, and wore an air of trembling consciousness. Sir Charles smiled again. He knew the sex; at least he said so. (It is an assertion often ventured upon.) Accordingly Sir Charles determined to come down from his height, and court nature and innocence in their own tones. This he rightly judged must be the proper course to take with Mrs. Vane. He fell down with mock ardor upon one knee.

The supposed Mrs. Vane gave a little squeak.

"Dear Mrs. Vane," cried he, "be not alarmed;

loveliness neglected, and simplicity deceived, ir sure respect, as well as adoration. Ah!" (A sigh.)

"O, get up, sir; do, please. Ah!" (A sigh.)

"You sigh, sweetest of human creatures. Ah why did not a nature like yours fall into hands that would have cherished it as it deserves? Had Heaven bestowed on me this hand, which I take ——"

"O, please, sir ——"

"With the profoundest respect, would I have abandoned such a treasure for an actress? — a Woffington! as artificial and hollow a jade as ever winked at a side box!"

"Is she, sir?"

"Notorious, madam. Your husband is the only man in London who does not see through her. How different are you! Even I, who have no taste for actresses, found myself revived, refreshed, ameliorated by that engaging picture of innocence and virtue you drew this morning; yourself the bright and central figure. Ah, dear angel! I remember all your favorites, and envy them their place in your recollections. Your Barbary mare ——"

"Hen, sir!"

"Of course I meant hen; and Gray Gillian, his old nurse ——"

"No, no, no! she is the mare, sir. He! he! he!"

"So she is. And Dame — Dame ——"

"Best!"

"Ah! I knew it. You see how I remember them all. And all carry me back to those innocent days which fleet too soon — days when an angel like you might have weaned me from the wicked pleasures of the town to the placid delights of a rural existence!"

"Alas, sir!"

"You sigh. It is not yet too late. I am a convert to you; I swear it on this white hand. Ah! how can I relinquish it, pretty fluttering prisoner?"

"O, sir, please ——"

"Stay a while."

"No! please, sir ——"

"While I fetter thee with a worthy manacle." Sir Charles slipped a diamond ring of great value upon his pretty prisoner.

"La, sir, how pretty!" cried innocence.

Sir Charles then undertook to prove that th lustre of the ring was faint, compared with tha of the present wearer's eyes. This did not sui innocence; she hung her head and fluttered, and showed a bashful repugnance to look her admirer in the face. Sir Charles playfully insisted, and Mrs. Woffington was beginning to be a little at a loss, when suddenly voices were heard upon the stairs.

"*My husband!*" cried the false Mrs. Vane; and in a moment she rose, and darted into Triplet's inner apartment.

Mr. Vane and Mr. Triplet were talking ear nestly as they came up the stair. It seems the wise Triplet had prepared a little dramatic scene for his own refreshment, as well as for the ultimate benefit of all parties. He had persuaded Mr. Vane to accompany him by warm, mysterious promises of a happy *dénouement;* and now, having conducted that gentleman as far as his door, he was heard to say, —

"And now, sir, you shall see one who waits to forget grief, suspicion — all, in your arms. Behold!" and here he flung the door open.

"The devil!"

"You flatter me!" said Pomander, who had had time to recover his *aplomb*, somewhat shaken, at first, by Mr. Vane's inopportune arrival.

Now, it is to be observed that Mr. Vane had not long ago seen his wife lying on her bed, to all appearance incapable of motion.

Mr. Vane, before Triplet could recover his surprise, inquired of Pomander why he had sent for him. "And what," added he, "is the grief — suspicion, I am, according to Mr. Triplet, to forget in your arms?"

Mr. Vane added this last sentence in rather a testy manner.

"Why, the fact is ——" began Sir Charles, without the remotest idea of what the fact was going to be.

"That Sir Charles Pomander ——" interrupted Triplet.

"But Mr. Triplet is going to explain," said Sir Charles, keenly.

"Nay, sir; be yours the pleasing duty. But now I think of it," resumed Triplet, "why not tell the simple truth? — it is not a play! She I brought you here to see was not Sir Charles Pomander; but ——"

"I forbid you to complete the name!" crie Pomander.

"I command you to complete the name!" cried Vane.

"Gentlemen, gentlemen! how can I do both?" remonstrated Triplet.

"Enough, sir!" cried Pomander. "It is a lady's secret. I am the guardian of that lady's honor."

"She has chosen a strange guardian of her honor?" said Vane, bitterly.

"Gentlemen!" cried poor Triplet, who did not at all like the turn things were taking, "I give you my word, she does not even know of Sir Charles's presence here!"

"Who?" cried Vane, furiously. "Man alive! who are you speaking of?"

"Mrs. Vane!"

"My wife!" cried Vane, trembling with anger and jealousy. "She here! — and with this man?"

"No!" cried Triplet. "With me, with me! Not with him, of course."

"Boaster!" cried Vane, contemptuously. "But that is a part of your profession!"

Pomander, irritated, scornfully drew from his ocket the ladies' joint production, which had allen at his feet from Mrs. Woffington's hand. Ie presented this to Mr. Vane, who took it very ıneasily; a mist swam before his eyes as he read :he words "Alone and unprotected — Mabel Vane." He had no sooner read these words, than he found he loved his wife: when he tampered with his treasure, he did not calculate on another seeking it.

This was Pomander's hour of triumph! He proceeded coolly to explain to Mr. Vane, that Mrs. Woffington having deserted him for Mr. Vane, and Mr. Vane his wife for Mrs. Woffington, the bereaved parties had, according to custom, agreed to console each other.

This soothing little speech was interrupted by Mr. Vane's sword flashing suddenly out of its sheath; while that gentleman, white with rage and jealousy, bade him instantly to take to his guard, or be run through the body like some noxious animal.

Sir Charles drew his sword, and in spite of Triplet's weak interference, half a dozen passes were rapidly exchanged, when suddenly the door of the inner room opened, and a lady in a hoo(pronounced, in a voice which was an excellen imitation of Mrs. Vane's, the word "False!"

The combatants lowered their points.

"You hear, sir!" cried Triplet.

"You see, sir!" said Pomander.

"Mabel!—wife!" cried Mr. Vane, in agony "O! say this is not true!—O! say that letter is a forgery! Say, at least, it was by some treachery you were lured to this den of iniquity! O! speak!"

The lady silently beckoned to some person inside.

"You know I loved you!—you know how bitterly I repent the infatuation that brought me to the feet of another!"

The lady replied not, though Vane's soul appeared to hang upon her answer. But she threw the door open, and there appeared another lady, the real Mrs. Vane! Mrs. Woffington then threw off her hood, and to Sir Charles Pomander's consternation, revealed the features of that ingenious person, who seemed born to outwit him.

"You heard that fervent declaration, mad-n?" said she to Mrs. Vane. "I present to you, ıadam, a gentleman, who regrets that he ever ıistook the real direction of his feelings. And ɔ you, sir," continued she, with great dignity, ' I present a lady, who will never mistake either ıer feelings or her duty."

"Ernest! dear Ernest!" cried Mrs. Vane, ɔlushing, as if she was the culprit. And she came forward, all love and tenderness.

Her truant husband kneeled at her feet of course. No! He said rather sternly, "How came you here, Mabel?"

"Mrs. Vane," said the actress, "fancied you had mislaid that weathercock, your heart, in Covent Garden, and that an actress had seen in it a fit companion for her own, and had feloniously appropriated it. She came to me to inquire after it."

"But this letter, signed by you?" said Vane, still addressing Mabel.

"Was written by me on a paper which accidentally contained Mrs. Vane's name. The fact is, Mr. Vane — I can hardly look you in the face — I had a little wager with Sir Charles here; his diamond ring — which you may see has become my diamond ring," (a horribly w. face from Sir Charles,) "against my left glov that I could bewitch a country gentleman's ir agination, and make him think me an ange Unfortunately the owner of his heart appeare(and like poor Mr. Vane, took our play for ea] nest. It became necessary to disabuse her, an to open your eyes. Have I done so?"

"You have, madam," said Vane, wincing a each word she said. But at last, by a mighty effort, he mastered himself, and coming to Mrs Woffington with a quivering lip, he held out his hand suddenly in a very manly way. "I have been the dupe of my own vanity," said he, "and I thank you for this lesson." Poor Mrs. Wof fington's fortitude had well nigh left her at this

"Mabel," he cried, "is this humiliation any punishment for my folly? any guaranty for my repentance? Can you forgive me?"

"It is all forgiven, Ernest. But, O! you are mistaken." She glided to Mrs. Woffington. "What do we not owe you, sister?" whispered she.

"Nothing! that word pays all," was the reply. She then slipped her address into Mrs. Vane's and, and courtesying to all the company, she hastily left the room.

Sir Charles Pomander followed; but he was not quick enough; she got a start, and purposely avoided him, and for three days neither the public nor private friends saw this poor woman's face.

Mr. and Mrs. Vane prepared to go also; but Mrs. Vane would thank good Mr. Triplet and Mrs. Triplet for their kindness to her.

Triplet the benevolent blushed, was confused and delighted; but suddenly turning somewhat sorrowful, he said, "Mr. Vane, madam, made use of an expression which caused a momentary pang He called this a den of iniquity. Now, this is my studio! But never mind."

Mr. Vane asked his pardon for so absurd an error, and the pair left Triplet in all the enjoyment which does come now and then to an honest man, whether this dirty little world will or not.

A coach was called, and they went home to Bloomsbury. Few words were said; but the repentant husband often silently pressed this angel to his bosom, and the tears which found their way to her beautiful eyelashes were tears o joy.

This weakish, and consequently villanous though not ill-disposed person would have gon down to Willoughby that night; but his wife hac great good sense. She would not take her husband off, like a schoolboy caught out of bounds She begged him to stay while she made certain purchases; but for all that, her heart burned to be at home. So in less than a week after the events we have related, they left London.

Meantime, every day Mrs. Vane paid a quiet visit to Mrs. Woffington (for some days the actress admitted no other visitor,) and was with her but two hours before she left London. On that occasion she found her very sad.

"I shall never see you again in this world," said she; "but I beg of you to write to me, that my mind may be in contact with yours."

She then asked Mabel, in her half-sorrowful, half-bitter way, how many months it would be ere she was forgotten.

Mabel answered by quietly crying. So then they embraced; and Mabel assured her friend she was not one of those who change their minds. "It is for life, dear sister; it is for life," cried she.

"Swear this to me," said the other, almost sternly. "But no. I have more confidence in that candid face and pure nature than in a human being's oath. If you are happy, remember you owe me something. If you are unhappy, come to me, and I will love you as men cannot love."

Then vows passed between them, for a singular tie bound these two women; and then the actress showed a part at least of her sore heart to her new sister; and that sister was surprised and grieved, and pitied her truly and deeply, and they wept on each other's neck; and at last they were fain to part. They parted; and true it was, they never met again in this world. They parted in sorrow; but when they meet again, it shall be with joy.

Women are generally such faithless, unscrupulous, and pitiless humbugs in their dealings with their own sex — which, whatever they may say, they despise at heart — that I am happy to be able to say, Mrs. Vane proved true as steel. She was a noble-minded, simple-hearted creature;

she was also a constant creature. Constancy is rare, a beautiful, a godlike virtue.

Four times every year she wrote a long lette: to Mrs. Woffington; and twice a year, in the cold weather, she sent her a hamper of country delicacies, that would have victualled a small garrison. And when her sister left this earthly scene — a humble, pious, long-repentant Christian — Mrs. Vane wore mourning for her, and sorrowed over her; but not as those who cannot hope to meet again.

My story as a work of art — good, bad, or indifferent — ends with that last sentence. If a reader accompanies me farther, I shall feel flattered, and he does so at his own risk.

My reader knows that all this befell long ago. That Woffington is gay and Triplet sad no more. That Mabel's, and all the bright eyes of that day, have long been dim, and all its cunning voices hushed. Judge then whether I am one of those happy story tellers who can end with a wedding. No! this story must wind up, as yours and mine ıust — to-morrow — or to-morrow — or to-morow! when our little sand is run.

Sir Charles Pomander lived a man of pleasure ıntil sixty. He then became a man of pain; he lragged the chain about eight years, and died miserably.

Mr. Cibber not so much died as "slipped his wind" — a nautical expression, that conveys the idea of an easy exit. He went off quiet and genteel. He was past eighty, and had lived fast His servant called him at seven in the morning. "I will shave at eight," said Mr. Cibber. John brought the hot water at eight; but his master had taken advantage of this interval in his toilet, to die! — to avoid shaving?

Snarl and Soaper conducted the criticism of their day with credit and respectability until a good old age, and died placidly a natural death, like twaddle, sweet or sour.

The Triplets, while their patroness lived, did pretty well. She got a tragedy of his accepted at her theatre. She made him send her a copy, and with her scissors cut out about half; sometimes thinning, sometimes cutting bodily away But, lo! the inherent vanity of Mr. Triplet came out strong. Submissively, but obstinately, I fought for the discarded beauties. Unluckily, h did this one day that his patroness was in one o her bitter humors. So she instantly gave hin back his manuscript, with a sweet smile ownec herself inferior in judgment to him, and left hin unmolested.

Triplet breathed freely; a weight was taken off him. The savage steel (he applied this title to the actress's scissors) had spared his *purpurei panni.* He was played, pure and intact, a calamity the rest of us grumbling escape.

But it did so happen that the audience were of the actress's mind, and found the words too exuberant, and the business of the play too scanty in proportion. At last their patience was so sorely tried that they supplied one striking incident to a piece deficient in facts. They gave the manager the usual broad hint, and in the middle of Triplet's third act a huge veil of green baize descended upon "The Jealous Spaniard."

Failing here, Mrs. Woffington contrived often to befriend him in his other arts; and, moreover, she often sent Mr. Triplet, what she called a snug investment, a loan of ten pounds, to be repaid at oomsday, with interest and compound interest, ccording to the Scriptures; and although she ıughed, she secretly believed she was to get her en pounds back, double and treble. And I beieve so too.

Some years later Mrs. Triplet became eventful. She fell ill, and lay a dying; but one fine morning, after all hope had been given up, she suddenly rose and dressed herself. She was quite well in body now, but insane.

She continued in this state a month, and then by God's mercy she recovered her reason; but now the disease fell another step, and lighted upon her temper — a more athletic vixen was not to be found. She had spoiled Triplet for this by being too tame; so when the dispensation came they sparred daily. They were now thoroughly unhappy. They were poor as ever, and their benefactress was dead, and they had learned to snap. A speculative tour had taken this pair to Bristol, then the second city in England. They sojourned in the suburbs.

One morning the postman brought a letter for Triplet, who was showing his landlord's boy how to plant onions. (N. B. Triplet had never planted an onion, but he was one of your *a priori* gen tlemen, and could show any body how to do any thing.) Triplet held out his hand for the letter but the postman held out his hand for half a crown first. Trip's profession had transpired and his clothes inspired diffidence. Triplet appealed to his good feeling.

He replied with exultation, that "he had none left." (A middle-aged postman, no doubt.)

Triplet then suddenly started from entreaty to King Cambyses' vein. In vain!

Mrs. Triplet came down, and essayed the blandishments of the softer sex. In vain! And as there were no assets, the postman marched off down the road.

Mrs. Triplet glided after him like an assassin, beckoning on Triplet, who followed, doubtful of her designs. Suddenly (truth compels me to relate this) she seized the obdurate official from behind, pinned both his arms to his side, and with her nose furiously telegraphed her husband.

He, animated by her example, plunged upon the man, and tore the letter from his hand, and opened it before his eyes.

It happened to be a very windy morning, and

when he opened the letter, an enclosure, printed on much finer paper, was caught into the air, and went down the wind. Triplet followed in kangaroo leaps, like a dancer making a flying exit.

The postman cried on all good citizens for help. Some collected and laughed at him; Mrs Triplet explaining that they were poor, and could not pay half a crown for the freight of half an ounce of paper. She held him convulsively until Triplet reappeared.

That gentleman on his return was ostentatiously calm and dignified. "You are, or were, in perturbation about half a crown," said he. "There sir, is a twenty pound note; oblige me with nineteen pounds, seventeen shillings, and sixpence. Should your resources be unequal to such a demand, meet me at the 'Green Cat and Brown Frogs' after dinner, when you shall receive your half crown, and drink another upon the occasion of my sudden accession to unbounded affluence."

The postman was staggered by the sentence, and overawed by the note, and chose the "Cat and Frogs," and liquid half crown.

Triplet took his wife down the road and

showed her the letter and enclosure. The letter ran thus: —

"Sir: We beg respectfully to inform you that our late friend and client, James Triplet, merchant, of the Minories, died last August, without a will, and that you are his heir.

"His property amounts to about twenty thousand pounds, besides some reversions. Having possessed the confidence of your late uncle, we should feel honored and gratified if you should think us worthy to act professionally for yourself.

"We enclose twenty pounds, and beg you will draw upon us as far as five thousand pounds, should you have immediate occasion.

We are, sir,

Your humble servants,

JAMES & JOHN ALLMITT.'

It was some time before these children of misfortune could realize this enormous stroke of compensation; but, at last, it worked its way into their spirits, and they began to sing, to triumph, and dance upon the king's highway.

Mrs. Triplet was the first to pause, and take etter views.

"O James!" she cried, "we have suffered auch! We have been poor, but honest, and the Almighty has looked upon us at last!"

Then they began to reproach themselves.

"O James! I have been a peevish woman — an ill wife to you, this many years!"

"No, no!" cried Triplet, with tears in his eyes. "It is I who have been rough and brutal! Poverty tried us too hard; but we were not like the rest of them — we were always faithful to the altar. And the Almighty has seen us, though we often doubted it."

"I never doubted that, James."

So then the poor things fell on their knees upon the public road, and thanked God. If any man had seen them, he would have said they were mad. Yet madder things are done every day, by gentlemen with faces as grave as the parish bull's. And then they rose, and formed their little plans.

Triplet was for devoting four fifths to charity, and living like a prince on the remainder. But Mrs. Triplet thought the poor were entitled to no more than two thirds, and they themselves ougl to bask in a third, to make up for what they ha gone through; and then suddenly she sighed and burst into tears.

"Lucy! Lucy!" sobbed she.

Yes, reader, God had taken little Lucy And her mother cried to think all this wealth and comfort had come too late for her darling child.

"Do not cry. Lucy is richer, a thousand times, than you are, with your twenty thousand pounds."

Their good resolutions were carried out, for a wonder. Triplet lived for years, the benefactor of all the loose fish that swim in and round theatres; and indeed the unfortunate seldom appealed to him in vain. He now predominated over the arts, instead of climbing them. In his latter day he became an oracle, as far as the science of acting was concerned; and, what is far more rare, he really got to know *something* about it. This was owing to two circumstances: first, he ceased to run blindfold in a groove behind the scenes; second, he became a frequenter of the first row of the pit, and that is where ie whole critic, and two thirds of the true actor, s made.

On one point, to his dying day, his feelings guided his judgment. He never could see an actress equal to his Woffington. Mrs. Abington was grace personified, but so was Woffington, said the old man. And Abington's voice is thin, Woffington's was sweet and mellow. When Jordan rose, with her voice of honey, her dewy freshness, and her heavenly laugh, that melted in along with her words, like the gold in the quartz, Triplet was obliged to own her the goddess of beautiful gayety; but still he had the last word: "Woffington was all *she* is, except her figure. Woffington was a Hebe — your Nell Jordan is little better than a dowdy."

Triplet almost reached the present century. He passed through great events, but they did not excite him; his eye was upon the arts. When Napoleon drew his conquering sword on England, Triplet's remark was, "Now we shall be driven upon native talent, thank Heaven!" The storms of Europe shook not Triplet. The fact is, nothing that happened on the great stage of the world seemed real to him. He believed in nothing, where there was no curtain visible. But even tl grotesque are not good in vain. Many an ey was wet round his dying bed, and many a tea fell upon his grave. He made his final exit i the year of grace 1799. And I, who laugh a him, would leave this world to-day, to be witl him; for I am tossing at sea — he is in port.

A straightforward character like Mabel's becomes a firm character with years. Long ere she was forty, her hand gently but steadily ruled Willoughby House — and all in it. She and Mr. Vane lived very happily; he gave her no fresh cause for uneasiness. Six months after their return, she told him what burned in that honest heart of hers, the truth about Mrs. Woffington. The water rushed to his eyes, but his heart was now wholly his wife's; and gratitude to Mrs. Woffington for her noble conduct was the only sentiment awakened.

"You must repay her, dearest," said he. "I know you love her, and until to-day it gave me ain; now it gives me pleasure. We owe her much."

The happy, innocent life of Mabel Vane is soon summed up. Frank as the day, constant as the sun, pure as the dew, she passed the golden years preparing herself and others for a still brighter eternity. At home, it was she who warmed and cheered the house, and the hearth, more than all the Christmas fires. Abroad, she shone upon the poor like the sun. She led her beloved husband by the hand to heaven. She led her children the same road; and she was leading her grandchildren when the angel of death came for her; and she slept in peace.

Many remember her. For she alone, of all our tale, lived in this present century; but they speak of her as "old Madam Vane," her whom we knew so young and fresh.

She lies in Willoughby Church — her mortal part; her spirit is with the spirits of our mothers and sisters, reader, that are gone before us; with the tender mothers, the chaste wives, the loyal friends, and the just women of all ages.

I come to her last, who went first; but I coul not have staid by the others, when once I ha laid my darling asleep. It seemed for a while a if the events of our tale did her harm; but it wa not so in the end.

Not many years afterwards, she was engaged by Mr. Sheridan, at a very heavy salary, and went to Dublin. Here the little girl, who had often carried a pitcher on her head down to the Liffey, and had played Polly Peachum in a booth, became a lion; dramatic, political, and literary, and the centre of the wit of that wittiest of cities.

But the Dublin ladies and she did not coalesce. They said she was a naughty woman, and not fit for them morally. She said they had but two topics, "silks and scandal," and were unfit for her intellectually.

This was the saddest part of her history. But it is darkest just before sunrise. She returned to London. Not long after, it so happened, that she went to a small church in the city one Sunday afternoon. The preacher was such as we have often heard; but not so this poor woman, in her day of sapless theology, ere John Wesley waked the ıoring church. Instead of sending a dry clat- ꞅr of morality about their ears, or evaporating ıe Bible in the thin generalities of the pulpit, his man drove God's truths home to the hearts ›f men and women. In his hands the divine ᵣirtues were thunderbolts, not swans' down. With good sense, plain speaking, and a heart yearning for the souls of his brethren and his sisters, he stormed the bosoms of many; and this afternoon, as he reasoned like Paul of righteousness, temperance, and judgment to come, sinners trembled — and Margaret Woffington was of those who trembled.

After this day she came ever to the narrow street where shone this house of God; and still, new light burst upon her heart and conscience. Here she learned why she was unhappy; here she learned how alone she could be happy; here she learned to know herself; and the moment she knew herself, she abhorred herself, and repented in dust and ashes.

This strong and straightforward character made no attempt to reconcile two things that an average Christian would have continued to reconcile. Her interest fell in a moment before her new sense of right. She flung her profession fro: her like a poisonous weed.

Long before this Mrs. Vane had begged her t leave the stage. She had replied, that it was t her what wine is to weak stomachs. "But, added she, "do not fear that I will ever craw down hill, and unravel my own reputation; noı will I ever do as I have seen others — stanc groaning at the wing, to go on giggling, and come off gasping. No! the first night the boards do not spring beneath my feet, and the pulse of the public beat under my hand, I am gone! Next day, at rehearsal, instead of Woffington, a note will come, to tell the manager that henceforth Woffington is herself — at Twickenham, or Richmond, or Harrow-on-the-Hill — far from his dust, his din, and his glare — quiet, till God takes her; amidst grass, and flowers, and charitable deeds."

This day had not come: it was in the zenith of her charms and her fame that she went home one night, after a play, and never entered a theatre, by front door or back door, again. She declined all leave-taking and ceremony.

"When a publican shuts up shop and ceases

diffuse liquid poison, he does not invite the orld to put up the shutters; neither will I. ctors overrate themselves ridiculously," added ie; "I am not of that importance to the world, or the world to me. I fling away a dirty old love instead of soiling my fingers filling it with nore guineas, and the world loses in me, what? mother old glove, full of words; half of them dle, the rest wicked, untrue, silly, or impure. *Rougissons, taisons-nous, et partons.*"

She now changed her residence, and withdrew politely from her old associates, courting two classes only, the good and the poor. She had always supported her mother and sister; but now charity became her system. The following is characteristic: —

A gentleman who had greatly admired this dashing actress, met one day, in the suburbs, a lady in an old black silk gown and a gray shawl, with a large basket on her arm. She showed him its contents — worsted stockings of prodigious thickness — which she was carrying to some of her *protégés*.

"But surely that is a waste of your valuable

time," remonstrated her admirer. "Much bett buy them."

"But, my good soul," replied the represent tive of Sir Harry Wildair, "you can't buy ther Nobody in this wretched town can knit worste hose except Woffington."

Conversions like this are open to just susp cion, and some did not fail to confound her wit certain great sinners, who have turned auster self-deceivers when sin smiled no more. Bu this was mere conjecture. The facts were clear, and speaking to the contrary. This woman left folly at its brightest, and did not become austere: on the contrary, though she laughed less, she was observed to smile far oftener than before. She was a humble and penitent, but cheerful, hopeful Christian.

Another class of detractors took a somewhat opposite ground: they accused her of bigotry, for advising a young female friend against the stage as a business. But let us hear herself. This is what she said to the girl: —

"At the bottom of my heart, I always loved and honored virtue. Yet the tendencies of the stage so completely overcame my good sentiɜnts, that I was for years a worthless woman. is a situation of uncommon and incessant mptation. Ask yourself, my child, whether ɩere is nothing else you can do, but this. It is, think, our duty and our wisdom to fly tempta- on whenever we can, as it is to resist it when ɾe cannot escape it."

Was this the tone of bigotry?

Easy in fortune, penitent, but cheerful, Mrs. Woffington had now but one care — to efface the memory of her former self, and to give as many years to purity and piety as had gone to folly and frailty. This was not to be. The Almighty did not permit, or perhaps I should say, did not require this.

Some unpleasant symptoms had long attracted her notice, but in the bustle of her profession had received little attention. She was now persuaded by her own medical attendant to consult Dr. Bowdler, who had a great reputation, and had been years ago an acquaintance and an admirer. He visited her; he examined her by means little used in that day, and he saw at once that her days were numbered.

Dr. Bowdler's profession and experience had

not steeled his heart as they generally do a: must do. He could not tell her this sad new: so he asked her for pen and paper, and said, " will write a prescription to Mr. ——." He the wrote, not a prescription, but a few lines, beggin Mr. —— to convey the cruel intelligence by de grees, and with care and tenderness. "It is al we can do for her," said he.

He looked so grave while writing the supposed prescription, that it unluckily occurred to Mrs. Woffington to look over him. She stole archly behind him, and, with a smile on her face,— read her death warrant.

It was a cruel stroke! A gasping sigh broke from her. At this Dr. Bowdler looked up, and to his horror saw the sweet face he had doomed to the tomb looking earnestly and anxiously at him, and very pale and grave. He was shocked, and strange to say, she, whose death warrant he had signed, ran and brought him a glass of wine, for he was quite overcome. Then she gave him her hand in her own sweet way, and bade him not grieve for her, for she was not afraid to die, and had long learned that "life is a walking shadow, a poor poor player, who frets and struts

.s hour upon the stage, and then is heard no .ore."

But no sooner was the doctor gone than she ʼept bitterly. Poor soul! she had set her heart .pon living as many years to God as she had to he world, and she had hoped to wipe out her :ormer self.

"Alas!" she said to her sister, "I have done more harm than I can ever hope to do good now; and my long life of folly and wickedness will be remembered — will be what they call famous; my short life of repentance who will know, or heed, or take to profit?"

But she soon ceased to repine. She bowed to the will of Heaven, and set her house in order, and awaited her summons. The tranquillity of her life and her courageous spirit were unfavorable to the progress of disease, and I am glad to say she was permitted to live nearly three years after this; and these three years were the happiest period of her whole life. Works of piety and love made the days eventful. She was at home now — she had never been at home in folly and loose living. All her bitterness was gone now, with its cause.

Reader, it was with her as it is with many a autumn day. Clouds darken the sun, rain an wind sweep over all, till day declines; but the comes one heavenly hour, when all ill thing seem spent. There is no more wind, no mor rain. The great sun comes forth, not fiery brigh indeed, but full of tranquil glory, and warms th sky with ruby waves, and the hearts of men with hope, as parting with us for a little space, he glides slowly and peacefully to rest.

So fared it with this humble, penitent, and now happy Christian.

A part of her desire was given her. She lived long enough to read a firm recantation of her former self, to show the world a great repentance, and to leave upon indelible record one more proof, what alone is true wisdom, and where alone true joys are to be found.

She endured some physical pain, as all must who die in their prime. But this never wrung a sigh from her great heart; and within she had the peace of God, which passes all understanding.

I am not strong enough to follow her to her last hour; nor is it needed. Enough that her vn words came true. When the great summons came, it found her full of hope, and peace, ıd joy; sojourning, not dwelling, upon earth; ır from dust, and din, and vice; the Bible in her and, the cross in her heart; quiet; amidst rass, and flowers, and charitable deeds.

"NON OMNEM MORITURAM."

THE END.

BOSTON, 135 WASHINGTON STREET.
JULY, 1855.

NEW BOOKS AND NEW EDITIONS

PUBLISHED BY

ICKNOR AND FIELDS.

THOMAS DE QUINCEY'S WRITINGS.

ONFESSIONS OF AN ENGLISH OPIUM-EATER, AND SUSPIRIA DE PROFUNDIS. With Portrait. Price 75 cents.

BIOGRAPHICAL ESSAYS. Price 75 cents.

MISCELLANEOUS ESSAYS. Price 75 cents.

THE CÆSARS. Price 75 cents.

LITERARY REMINISCENCES. 2 vols. Price $1.50.

NARRATIVE AND MISCELLANEOUS PAPERS. 2 vols. Price $1 50.

ESSAYS ON THE POETS, &c. 1 vol. 16mo. 75 cents.

HISTORICAL AND CRITICAL ESSAYS. 2 vols. $1.50.

AUTOBIOGRAPHIC SKETCHES. 1 vol. Price 75 cents.

ESSAYS ON PHILOSOPHICAL WRITERS, &c. 2 vols. 16mo. $1.50.

LETTERS TO A YOUNG MAN, AND OTHER PAPERS. 1 vol. Price 75 cents.

THEOLOGICAL ESSAYS AND OTHER PAPERS. 2 Vols. Price $1.50.

THE NOTE BOOK OF AN ENGLISH OPIUM EATER. 1 Vol. Price 75 cents.

ALFRED TENNYSON'S WRITINGS.

POETICAL WORKS. With Portrait. 2 vols. Cloth. $1.50.

THE PRINCESS. Boards. Price 50 cents.

IN MEMORIAM. Cloth. Price 75 cents.

HENRY W. LONGFELLOW'S WRITINGS.

THE GOLDEN LEGEND. A Poem. Just Publishe(Price $1.00.

POETICAL WORKS. This edition contains the six Vol umes mentioned below. In two volumes. 16mo. Boards $2.00.

In Separate Volumes, each 75 cents.

VOICES OF THE NIGHT.
BALLADS AND OTHER POEMS.
SPANISH STUDENT; A PLAY IN THREE ACTS.
BELFRY OF BRUGES, AND OTHER POEMS.
EVANGELINE: A TALE OF ACADIE.
THE SEASIDE AND THE FIRESIDE.
THE WAIF. A Collection of Poems. Edited by Longfellow.
THE ESTRAY. A Collection of Poems. Edited by Longfellow.

MR. LONGFELLOW'S PROSE WORKS.

HYPERION. A ROMANCE. Price $1.00.
OUTRE-MER. A PILGRIMAGE. Price $1.00.
KAVANAGH. A TALE. Price 75 cents.

Illustrated editions of EVANGELINE, POEMS, HYPERION, and THE GOLDEN LEGEND.

OLIVER WENDELL HOLMES'S WRITINGS.

POETICAL WORKS. With fine Portrait. Boards. $1.00.
ASTRÆA. Fancy paper. Price 25 cents.

BARRY CORNWALL'S WRITINGS.

ENGLISH SONGS AND OTHER SMALL POEMS. (Enlarged Edition. Price $1.00.
ESSAYS AND TALES IN PROSE. 2 Vols. Price $1.50.

NATHANIEL HAWTHORNE'S WRITINGS.

WICE-TOLD TALES. Two Volumes. Price $1.50.

HE SCARLET LETTER. Price 75 cents.

HE HOUSE OF THE SEVEN GABLES. Price $1.00.

'HE SNOW IMAGE, AND OTHER TWICE-TOLD TALES. Price 75 cents.

THE BLITHEDALE ROMANCE. Price 75 cents.

MOSSES FROM AN OLD MANSE. New Edition. 2 vols. Price $1.50.

TRUE STORIES FROM HISTORY AND BIOGRAPHY. With four fine Engravings. Price 75 cents.

A WONDER-BOOK FOR GIRLS AND BOYS. With seven fine Engravings. Price 75 cents.

TANGLEWOOD TALES. Another 'Wonder-Book.' With Engravings. Price 88 cents.

LIFE OF GEN. PIERCE. 1 vol. 16mo. Cloth. 50 cts.

JAMES RUSSELL LOWELL'S WRITINGS.

COMPLETE POETICAL WORKS. Revised, with Additions. In two volumes, 16mo. Cloth. Price $1.50.

SIR LAUNFAL. New Edition. Price 25 cents.

A FABLE FOR CRITICS. New Edition. Price 50 cents.

THE BIGLOW PAPERS. A New Edition. Price 63 cents.

EDWIN P. WHIPPLE'S WRITINGS.

ESSAYS AND REVIEWS. 2 Vols. Price $2.00

LECTURES ON SUBJECTS CONNECTED WITH LITERATURE AND LIFE. Price 63 cents.

WASHINGTON AND THE REVOLUTION. Price 20 cts.

JOHN G. WHITTIER'S WRITINGS.

OLD PORTRAITS AND MODERN SKETCHES. 75 cei
MARGARET SMITH'S JOURNAL. Price 75 cents.
SONGS OF LABOR, AND OTHER POEMS. Boards. 50 (
THE CHAPEL OF THE HERMITS. Cloth. 50 cents.
LITERARY RECREATIONS AND MISCELLANIE
Cloth. $1.00.

GEORGE S. HILLARD'S WRITINGS.

SIX MONTHS IN ITALY. 1 vol. 16mo. Price $1.50.
DANGERS AND DUTIES OF THE MERCANTIL
PROFESSION. Price 25 cents.

HENRY GILES'S WRITINGS.

LECTURES, ESSAYS, AND MISCELLANEOUS WRIT-
INGS. 2 vols. Price $1.50.
DISCOURSES ON LIFE. Price 75 cents.
ILLUSTRATIONS OF GENIUS. Cloth. $1.00.

R. H. STODDARD'S WRITINGS.

POEMS. Cloth. Price 63 cents.
ADVENTURES IN FAIRY LAND. Price 75 cents.

BAYARD TAYLOR'S WRITINGS.

ROMANCES, LYRICS AND SONGS. Cloth. Price 63 cts.
POEMS OF THE ORIENT. Cloth. 75 cents.

WILLIAM MOTHERWELL'S WRITINGS.

POEMS, NARRATIVE AND LYRICAL. New Ed. $1.25.
POSTHUMOUS POEMS. Boards. Price 50 cents.
MINSTRELSY, ANC. AND MOD. 2 Vols. Boards. $1.50.

MRS. MOWATT.

AUTOBIOGRAPHY OF AN ACTRESS. Price $1.25.
PLAYS. ARMAND AND FASHION. Price 50 cents.

GOETHE'S WRITINGS.

ILHELM MEISTER. Translated by THOMAS CARLYLE. 2 Vols. Price $2.50.

OETHE'S FAUST. Translated by HAYWARD. Price 75 cts.

CAPT. MAYNE REID'S JUVENILE BOOKS.

HE DESERT HOME, OR, THE ADVENTURES OF A LOST FAMILY IN THE WILDERNESS. With fine Plates, $1.00

THE BOY HUNTERS. With fine Plates. Just published. Price 75 cents.

THE YOUNG VOYAGEURS, OR, THE BOY HUNTERS IN THE NORTH. With Plates. Price 75 cents.

THE FOREST EXILES. With fine Plates. 75 cents.

GRACE GREENWOOD'S WRITINGS.

GREENWOOD LEAVES. 1st & 2d Series. $1.25 each.

POETICAL WORKS. With fine Portrait. Price 75 cents.

HISTORY OF MY PETS. With six fine Engravings. Scarlet cloth. Price 50 cents.

RECOLLECTIONS OF MY CHILDHOOD. With six fine Engravings. Scarlet cloth. Price 50 cents.

HAPS AND MISHAPS OF A TOUR IN EUROPE. Price $1.25.

MERRIE ENGLAND. A new Juvenile. Price 75 cents.

MARY RUSSELL MITFORD'S WRITINGS.

OUR VILLAGE. Illustrated. 2 Vols. 16mo. Price $2.50.

ATHERTON, AND OTHER STORIES. 1 Vol. 16mo. $1.25.

MRS. CROSLAND'S WRITINGS.

LYDIA: A WOMAN'S BOOK. Cloth. Price 75 cents.

ENGLISH TALES AND SKETCHES. Cloth. $1.00.

MEMORABLE WOMEN. Illustrated. $1.00.

ANNA MARY HOWITT.

AN ART STUDENT IN MUNICH. Price $1.25.

A SCHOOL OF LIFE. A Story. Price 75 cents.

MRS. JUDSON'S WRITINGS.

ALDERBROOK. By Fanny Forrester. 2 vols. Price $1.

THE KATHAYAN SLAVE, AND OTHER PAPEF 1 vol. Price 63 cents.

MY TWO SISTERS: A Sketch from Memory. Price 50 c

POETRY.

ALEXANDER SMITH'S POEMS. 1 Vol. 16mo. Clotl Price 50 cents.

CHARLES MACKAY'S POEMS. 1 Vol. Cloth. Price $1.00

ROBERT BROWNING'S Poetical Works. 2 Vols. $2.00.

HENRY ALFORD'S POEMS. Just out. Price $1.25.

RICHARD MONCKTON MILNES. Poems of Many Years. Boards. Price 75 cents.

CHARLES SPRAGUE. Poetical and Prose Writings. With fine Portrait. Boards. Price 75 cents.

GERMAN LYRICS. Translated by Charles T. Brooks. 1 vol. 16mo. Cloth. Price $1.00.

THOMAS W. PARSONS. Poems. Price $1.00.

ALICE CARY'S POEMS $1.00.

LYTERIA: A Dramatic Poem. Price 63 cents.

JOHN G. SAXE. Poems. With Portrait. Boards, 63 cents. Cloth, 75 cents.

HENRY T. TUCKERMAN. Poems. Cloth. Price 75 cents.

BOWRING'S MATINS AND VESPERS. Price 50 cents.

GEORGE LUNT. Lyric Poems, &c. 1 Vol. Cloth. 63 cts.

PHŒBE CAREY. Poems and Parodies. 75 cents.

MEMORY AND HOPE. A Book of Poems, referring to Childhood. Cloth. Price $2.00.

THALATTA: A Book for the Sea-Side. 1 vol. 16mo. Cloth. Price 75 cts.

PASSION-FLOWERS. 1 vol. 16mo. Price 75 cents.

YRIARTE'S FABLES. Translated by G. H. Devereux. Price 63 cents

MISCELLANEOUS.

RISTIE JOHNSTONE. By CHARLES READE. Price 75 cts.

G WOFFINGTON. By CHARLES READE. Price 75 cents.

:NSLEY: A STORY WITHOUT A MORAL. Price 75 cts.

SAYS ON THE FORMATION OF OPINIONS AND THE PURSUIT OF TRUTH. 1 vol. 16mo. Price $1.00.

ALDEN: OR, LIFE IN THE WOODS. By HENRY D. THOREAU. 1 vol. 16mo. Price $1.00.

GHT ON THE DARK RIVER: OR, MEMOIRS OF MRS. HAMLIN. 1 vol. 16mo. Cloth. Price $1.00.

HE BARCLAYS OF BOSTON. BY MRS. H. G. OTIS. 1 vol. 12mo. $1.25.

OTES FROM LIFE. BY HENRY TAYLOR, author of 'Philip Van Artevelde.' 1 vol. 16mo. Cloth. Price 63 cents.

:EJECTED ADDRESSES. By HORACE and JAMES SMITH. Boards, Price 50 cents. Cloth, 63 cents.

VARRENIANA. A Companion to the 'Rejected Addresses.' Price 63 cents.

WILLIAM WORDSWORTH'S BIOGRAPHY. 2 vols. $2.50.

ART OF PROLONGING LIFE. By HUFELAND. Edited by ERASMUS WILSON, F. R. S. 1 vol. 16mo. Price 75 cents.

JOSEPH T. BUCKINGHAM'S PERSONAL MEMOIRS AND RECOLLECTIONS OF EDITORIAL LIFE. With Portrait. 2 vols. 16mo. Price $1.50.

VILLAGE LIFE IN EGYPT. By the Author of 'Purple Tints of Paris.' 2 vols. 16mo. Price $1.25.

DR. JOHN C. WARREN. The Preservation of Health, &c. 1 Vol. Price 38 cents.

PRIOR'S LIFE OF EDMUND BURKE. 2 vols. $2.00.

NATURE IN DISEASE. BY DR. JACOB BIGELOW. 1 vol. 16mo. Price $1.50.

CHARLES KINGSLEY. AMYAS LEIGH. An Historical Novel. 12 mo. Price $1.25.

WILLIAM HOWITT. A BOY'S ADVENTURES IN AUSTRALIA. 1 Vol. 16mo. Price 75 cents.

REV. CHARLES LOWELL, D. D. PRACTICAL SERMO
1 vol. 12mo. Price $1 25

PALISSY THE POTTER. By the Author of 'How to ma Home Unhealthy.' 2 vols. 16mo. Price $1.50.

WILLIAM MOUNTFORD. THORPE: A QUIET ENGLIS TOWN, AND HUMAN LIFE THEREIN. 16mo. Price $1.00.

MRS. A C. LOWELL. EDUCATION OF GIRLS. Price 25 cts.

CHARLES SUMNER. ORATIONS AND SPEECHES. 2 Vols Price $2.50.

HORACE MANN. THOUGHTS FOR A YOUNG MAN. 25 cents.

F. W. P. GREENWOOD. SERMONS OF CONSOLATION. $1.00.

MEMOIR OF THE BUCKMINSTERS, FATHER AND SON. By Mrs. LEE. Price $1.25

THE SOLITARY OF JUAN FERNANDEZ. By the Author of Picciola. Price 50 cents.

THE BOSTON BOOK. Price $1.25.

ANGEL-VOICES. Price 38 cents.

SIR ROGER DE COVERLEY. From the 'Spectator.' 75 cts.

S. T. WALLIS. SPAIN, HER INSTITUTIONS, POLITICS, AND PUBLIC MEN. Price $1.00.

MEMOIR OF ROBERT WHEATON. Price $1.00.

RUTH, A New Novel by the Author of 'MARY BARTON.' Cheap Edition. Price 38 cents.

LABOR AND LOVE: A TALE OF ENGLISH LIFE. 50 cents.

MRS. PUTNAM'S RECEIPT BOOK; AN ASSISTANT TO HOUSEKEEPERS. 1 vol. 16mo. Price 50 cents.

EACH OF THE ABOVE POEMS AND PROSE WRITINGS, MAY BE HAD IN VARIOUS STYLES OF HANDSOME BINDING.

☞ Any book published by TICKNOR & FIELDS, will be sent by mail, postage free, on receipt of the publication price.

Their stock of Miscellaneous Books is very complete, and they respectfully solicit orders from CITY AND COUNTRY LIBRARIES.

www.ingramcontent.com/pod-product-compliance
Lightning Source LLC
LaVergne TN
LVHW020234110826
845151LV00003B/923
9781425530600